# SOUTH ASIAN Folktales, myths & Legends

For my niece and nephew,
may your futures be
full of stories

## About the Author

Sarah Shaffi grew up devouring books,
reading at the dinner table, in bed and
when she was supposed to be doing
homework, searching for tales about
people like her. Now she is a journalist
and author and writes her own stories.

# SOUTH ASIAN
## Folktales, Myths & Legends

### SARAH SHAFFI

#### Illustrated by ABEEHA TARIQ

SCHOLASTIC

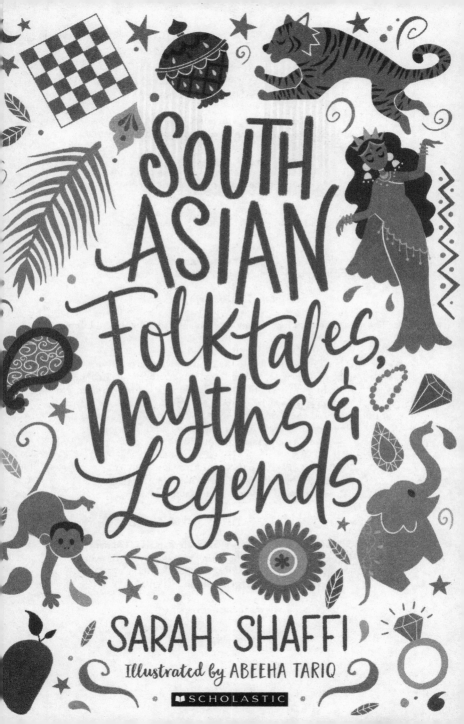

Published in the UK by Scholastic, 2022

1 London Bridge, London, SE1 9BA
Scholastic Ireland, 89E Lagan Road, Dublin Industrial Estate,
Glasnevin, Dublin, D11 HP5F

SCHOLASTIC and associated logos are trademarks and/or
registered trademarks of Scholastic Inc.

Text © Sarah Shaffi, 2022
Illustrations by Abeeha Tariq © Scholastic, 2022

The right of Sarah Shaffi to be identified
as the author of this work has been asserted by her
under the Copyright, Designs and Patents Act 1988.

ISBN 978 0702 31713 2

A CIP catalogue record for this book is available from the British Library.

Printed by CPI Group (UK) Ltd, Croydon, CR0 4YY
Papers used by Scholastic Children's Books are made
from wood grown in sustainable forests.

1 3 5 7 9 10 8 6 4 2

www.scholastic.co.uk

# Contents

## Royalty

# Introduction

Think about your favourite story. What happens in it? How does it make you feel? What is it about?

If you ask someone else who has read that same story those questions, their answers will probably be completely different. It might be because they've heard a different version, or it might be because everyone inhales stories in a different way. All of the stories in this book were told orally before they were written down, meaning that as they were passed from person to person they changed slightly. Sometimes people preferred to emphasize one thing over another; sometimes the tellers expanded on a part that particularly called to them.

As storytellers travelled, the stories travelled as well, across South Asia — a region comprising of Afghanistan, Bangladesh, Bhutan, India, the Maldives, Nepal, Pakistan and Sri Lanka. At the time the tales told in this collection originated, the world was very different. Countries that exist now did not exist then. Borders were in different places. There were empires that stretched across land and sea, reflected in stories like "The Three Princes", where the characters travel vast distances to what are now cities in India, Iran and Uzbekistan.

This means that when it comes to placing some stories, we can't be sure where they might have first been told; it also means that there are versions of the same story in a number of different countries. Some tales have even travelled beyond South Asia to East Asia, Europe and further!

Some of these stories – especially those with religious origins – were first written down hundreds of years ago, their writers unclear. Other stories were recorded in their most famous English versions more recently, and these were often done so by men, and largely white men, even though the originators of these tales would have been from very different backgrounds. This has resulted in stories that sometimes sideline women or that are told from the point of view of colonizers or that are sparse in the detail that would have made them rich and resulted in their original popularity.

In some cases, these tales weren't properly recorded or were only recorded briefly in English, meaning they're hard to access. This has been the case with stories from the Maldives, which has a rich tradition of folktales and myths. Among these is the story of why coconuts are so important in the country, which says that the first people on the islands were struggling to feed themselves, so a sorcerer came up with a plan. He used magic to grow coconut trees from the bodies of those who died, and then taught people how to use the trees for food and shelter. However, at some point, many of the traditional tales of the Maldives stopped being told as widely, which is why this tale has not been included in this collection. There are likely people in the Maldives today who know the folklore of the islands well; we can only hope they write their versions down so we can enjoy them in the future.

A lot of the stories in this collection, such as "Rama and Sita", or "Four Harmonious Friends", have been retold over and over and the stories in this book are a version of the original tales, told for today's world. They're written with respect for the source material, but like all stories that are retold, they are sometimes a little different to what's come before. And perhaps, just perhaps, some of these will go on to become your favourite stories, for you to interpret and retell.

# Animal Tales

Animals, from familiar creatures like cats to less well-known creatures like jackals, feature prominently in a lot of stories, but in the following they all take centre stage, acting like humans. Some of the stories here are fables: stories that convey a moral.

# The Lonely Crocodile

## (Sri Lanka)

*This story, originally called "The Crocodile's Wedding", features in Village Folk-Tales of Ceylon by Henry Parker. Parker was a British engineer who lived in Sri Lanka in the Victorian era, when it was colonized.*

In a vast lake on the edge of a jungle lived a crocodile. He was fearsome and tough and more than a little bit scary.

His big teeth frightened all who caught a glimpse of them when he grinned, and the snap his jaws made when he shut his mouth sent shudders through animals big and small. His leathery skin looked impenetrable, so no one ever tried to get the better of him.

Now, everyone had good reason to be scared of the crocodile. He *did* eat animals for breakfast, lunch and dinner, and he wasn't good at making friends, instead snapping at them when he talked, making them think he was going to eat them even if he wasn't. (To be fair to the animals, he usually *was* going to eat them.)

But, like all creatures, all the crocodile wanted was to be loved. Unfortunately, there were no other crocodiles who lived in his lake, and he didn't know anyone who could introduce him to another crocodile.

Until one day, a jackal appeared. The jackal was a cunning creature, one who kept his ear to the ground and always knew the latest goings-on almost as soon as they happened. News had reached him that an elephant had died on the opposite side of the large lake, and the jackal was keen to make a meal (or two, or three) of him. There was just one problem: the lake was big and the jackal couldn't swim that far.

The jackal, being the clever and cunning and gossip-loving animal he was, also knew that the crocodile really wanted someone to love and be loved by in return, so he decided to use this to his advantage.

Standing on the bank of the lake, far enough away that the crocodile couldn't catch him in the snap of his long jaw, the jackal called: "O Crocodile, Crocodile, where are you?"

The crocodile emerged slowly from the water. First just a few ridges from his back became visible. Then the tops of his eyes popped out of the water, and then his whole face emerged as he swam closer.

"What is it, Jackal?" asked the crocodile crossly. He'd been right in the middle of moping, and he wasn't really in the mood to talk to anyone.

The jackal smiled in a way he hoped seemed welcoming and open. "I have good news, Crocodile," he said. "Word has reached me that there might be a mate for you in another lake not far from here."

The crocodile immediately perked up. A partner? For him? Could it be true?

"There's just one problem," added the jackal. The crocodile's heart sank. Of course it was too good to be true. The jackal continued speaking, unaware of the emotions the crocodile was going through. "I cannot swim and so I have no way to get across the lake. If I could, I would happily go and see this other crocodile and see if the two of you are a match."

*Well, that,* thought the crocodile, *is something I can help with!*

"I can take you across the lake on my back," said the crocodile cheerily. "I'm a fast swimmer, and it will take no time at all. And you'll be above the water, so there's no chance of you getting wet."

The jackal didn't reply immediately, knowing that making the crocodile wait would make him more eager to help, and easier for the jackal to work with.

"Are you sure you won't eat me instead?" asked the jackal. "You do have a reputation, and I'll be at your mercy."

"I would never harm someone who was trying to help me!" exclaimed the crocodile. "I promise

I'll give you a ride over to the other side of the lake, and I'll bring you back at the end of the day safe and sound. No eating involved."

The jackal agreed and gingerly stepped forward and on to the crocodile's back. He took a couple of moments to settle himself down into a comfortable position. Then the crocodile swung around, and they were off.

The journey was pleasant — the water was smooth and the slight breeze in the air felt good on the jackal's fur. And all that fresh air only served to make the jackal hungrier.

Once the crocodile reached the other side, he indicated that the jackal should jump off. On the bank, the jackal turned to face the crocodile.

"I imagine it will take me some time to find this other crocodile," said the jackal. "And I'll need to talk to them properly. I'll meet you back here at dusk tonight and you can take me back over the lake."

The crocodile, full of anticipation and excitement, swam off for a day of frolicking in the lake. And the jackal headed off to find the elephant, which luckily wasn't too far from the water.

The elephant was huge, and the jackal ate

throughout the day, taking naps in between to help him digest the delicious meals.

As the sun began to set, there was still so much of the elephant left to eat, but the jackal knew he couldn't miss his lift back. So he made his way back to the lake, where the crocodile was waiting. "What happened?" asked the crocodile eagerly. "What happened? Have you found me a mate?"

"Take me back to the other side of the lake and we'll talk there," said the jackal. "It's been a long day and I've worked very hard, and I want to rest on the journey."

The jackal settled on to the crocodile's back and snoozed lightly on the way back. At the other side of the lake, he hopped off and turned to face the crocodile. "I have some good news and some bad news," he said. "I found the other crocodile family, which is the good news. But it took me almost all day, so I only got to briefly introduce myself to them. They want me to go back tomorrow to talk more."

"But that's all good news!" said the crocodile. "I'll happily take you back tomorrow, and hopefully now that you've found the other crocodiles, you can find me a mate."

The jackal nodded as though he was agreeing to do the crocodile a huge favour, but on the inside he was smirking widely; the crocodile had reacted exactly the way he wanted and now he could go back tomorrow and eat some more of that delicious elephant.

The pair agreed on a time to meet the next day, and the jackal padded back to his home where he comfortably slept the night away, full from his day of feasting. The crocodile didn't sleep well because he was so excited at the possibility of finding someone to love him at last, and so the next morning he was super early to meet the jackal.

As with the day before, the jackal hopped on to the crocodile's back for a peaceful trip across the lake. On the other side, the pair bid each other farewell and the crocodile went off to swim, while the jackal headed to have an early lunch of elephant.

Once more, the jackal spent the day eating and napping, and in the evening, when he met with the crocodile again, he climbed on to his back for the ride home. On the other side, the jackal hopped off and turned to face the crocodile.

"I had a very good chat with the crocodiles in the other lake today," said the jackal, watching as the crocodile smiled happily, all his sharp teeth on show. "There's definitely a match for you there, but I need to go back tomorrow to tie up some loose ends, and to arrange your meeting to see if you're compatible."

The crocodile was almost buzzing with excitement as he arranged a time to meet the jackal the next day. *This is it,* he thought, *I could finally meet someone I can spend my life with.*

On the third day, the journey over the lake was quieter than ever. The crocodile was too busy making a list of things he needed to do before he met the other crocodile (clean his teeth, sharpen his claws, have a long bath, tidy up his home, and so on) and the jackal was thinking about the feast ahead.

When the jackal reached the elephant, he saw that there wasn't much left to eat. Oh, there was still enough for a good day of food, but this would be his last trip over. Wasting no time, he got straight to it and, you guessed it, spent the day eating and napping.

The crocodile, as usual, arrived on time to meet the jackal for the journey back over, although the jackal couldn't help but notice that the crocodile looked a little bit more spruced up than usual.

When they reached the other side of the lake, the jackal hopped off and began to make his way into the jungle.

"Wait!" shouted the crocodile. "Is my possible future partner coming over to meet me tonight? I know you must be tired from a long day of talking, but if you just quickly tell me the details, I can do everything from here."

The jackal turned to face the crocodile, who looked eagerly back. "Ha," the jackal barked in laughter. "There is no other crocodile." He continued laughing as the crocodile looked at him, stunned.

"What do you mean?" asked the crocodile. "I've taken you over the lake three times now, and you've been speaking to the other crocodiles. Did they not like the sound of me?" The thought made the crocodile sad, even sadder than when he hadn't known about the other crocodiles and thought he was going to be alone for ever. Having the hope snatched away from him was worse.

The jackal was laughing so hard he almost couldn't speak, but he pulled himself together enough to explain. "There are no other crocodiles at all," he said to the crocodile. "I wasn't going over there to speak to anyone about you; I was going over there to feast on a delicious elephant, and you were just the lift I needed to get there."

The crocodile was stunned to find he'd been tricked, and he was overcome by a surge of anger. But it was too late. The jackal was no fool; he'd run into the jungle as soon as he'd finished his explanation, knowing the crocodile wouldn't be happy with him.

The crocodile snapped his teeth a few times, but he knew it was no use chasing after the jackal. Instead, he slunk back into the lake to brood.

And he never gave anyone a lift across the water ever again.

# The Fate of the Turtle

## (INDIA)

*This is from* The Olive Fairy Book *by Andrew Lang. Although it's a tale about keeping your word and about the things that are meant to be, it takes on new relevance now with its tale of rain shortages and changing weather.*

*Lang was a Scottish poet, novelist and literary critic, and he collected folk and fairy tales from around the world, publishing many books.*

Once upon a time, there was a beautiful lake in a hot country. Its waters were deep and still and clear, and everything around it grew lush and plentiful.

The lake was so attractive that one day two wild ducks happened upon it, and were so impressed that they decided to make it their home, even though originally they'd only been planning to stay for a couple of days.

Now, the lake was already home to a large, old turtle who had lived there for more years than can be counted on your fingers and toes many times over. The wild ducks were quite active and could be noisy, and the turtle was slow and preferred a quiet life. You would think that they would be quite at odds with each other.

But the turtle and wild ducks became close friends, spending lots of time together. Sometimes they sat quietly, other times they were more raucous.

Moons passed, and life was good. The ducks had plenty of water to splash about in and drink from, and the turtle was able to shelter in the shade from the trees that grew tall and leafy out of the water of the lake.

But soon, things began to change. At first, it was barely noticeable. It rained a little bit less, but everyone kept on living as before. Then the heat continued, and the ducks and the turtle noticed that it hadn't rained for weeks.

At first, the lake remained full, but soon some of the plants furthest away began to turn brown and die, because water was no longer reaching them through the earth.

Then the leaves of the trees closer to the lake began to shrivel up, and soon the mud on the banks of the lake became dry and turned into dirt. The lake got smaller and smaller and smaller.

The wild ducks had grown more worried over time, as the space for them to swim had decreased. Without a good-sized lake, they would soon be uncomfortable, and grow hungry.

One night, as they sheltered in their home, they had a serious conversation. "It might be time," said the first duck to the second. "If it doesn't rain within the next two days, we have to move on and find somewhere new to live."

The second duck nodded, gravely but in agreement. And then she had a thought. "But what about turtle? How will we tell him that we're going to leave him? He's our closest friend."

Both ducks pondered for a while, thinking about

how they would break the news to turtle. "We will just have to be honest," said the first duck. "And if it rains, we won't have to leave, so there might be nothing for us to worry about."

Over the next two days, the ducks anxiously watched the sky. But there wasn't any rain: not a downpour, not a shower, not even a sprinkle. Not one single drop of rain fell from the sky, and by now, the lake was tiny enough that the ducks could barely swim on it together. So they made their way to the turtle's home.

"Ooooohhh," yawned turtle. "I have had a most excellent nap, and I am very glad to see you both upon waking." Then he took in the serious faces of the ducks. "What is the matter?"

The ducks looked at each other, and then turned back to look at the turtle. The first duck spoke: "We've been waiting and waiting and waiting for rain, but none has come. We can't survive here for much longer…"

The first duck trailed off, too nervous to go on, so the second duck decided to speak up. "It's been a hard decision, and we don't want to leave you," she said, "but we have to find a new home with more water."

The turtle was stunned, and for a moment didn't know what to say. "But, but," he said. "But you're my closest friends, and if you leave I'll have no one." A tear slipped out of his eye and down his aged face. He had lived alone for many years, but now he knew what it was like to have friends, he didn't think he could go back to that lonely existence.

Both ducks were sniffling too, sad at the thought of leaving their friend, and at the sight of his tears. "We don't have a choice," the first duck said. "If we stay here, we won't survive."

"So take me with you!" the turtle exclaimed. "You cannot leave me here all alone without you. The lack of lake waters plus the lack of friendship means I won't survive either. I'm old anyway, and if you leave I'll die even more quickly."

"We plan to fly to find our new home," said the second duck. "And you can't fly. If we walk with you, we'll all be exhausted within a few hours, and we won't have made it anywhere. We need to find water first."

"But there must be something you can do," said the turtle. "Please, please. You're so clever, you can think of something."

The ducks weren't sure there was a solution, but

they promised the turtle they would try and think of something that night. They returned to their home, and spent hours coming up with ideas and then discarding them. Finally, very late at night, or very early in the morning, depending on how you look at it, they came up with a plan they thought would work.

The next morning, after a few short hours of sleep, the ducks walked along the edge of the now very small lake until they found what they were looking for. They carried everything they needed to the turtle's house and woke him up.

"Have you found a way to take me with you?" the turtle asked eagerly.

"Yes," said the first duck.

"But you must follow our instructions to the letter," said the second duck.

The turtle nodded eagerly in agreement, and so the ducks began to explain. "We will secure this big stick between us," said the first duck, gesturing to the stick they had brought with them, which they had found on the side of the lake. "You will hold on to the stick using your mouth, and that way we'll be able to fly with you."

"But," said the second duck. "You. Must. Not.

Let. Go. You must not open your mouth to talk or sigh or yawn. Whatever you do, you must hold on until we land. Do you understand?"

"Yes, yes," said the turtle. "I promise to hold on to the stick and not let go, whatever happens."

So, using some reeds, the ducks secured the stick between them. The turtle clamped on with his teeth, and then the ducks lifted up into the air.

What a thrill! The ducks moved quickly through the air, and the turtle had to do nothing but hold on and enjoy the scenery around him.

For a few hours, the ducks flew on, over forests and fields and small hills. Then, they began to fly over the edges of a village, and soon they were flying over dozens of houses.

The people of the village looked up, and were fascinated at the sight of the ducks flying with a turtle suspended from a stick between them. They pointed and smiled and laughed and cheered, and the children began to run under the ducks to try and keep up.

Now, until this point, the turtle had kept his promise. He'd held on, and not even opened his mouth when he felt the urge to yawn. But now, seeing how excited the children were, he wanted to talk to them. And so, he opened his mouth to shout hello to them.

And

he

fell.

He fell away from the ducks and down, down, down towards the villagers. Luckily, the children who had been running under the ducks were quick thinkers, and held out one of their scarves to catch the turtle.

But the fall had been so long for the turtle that he fell asleep on the way down, and didn't wake up again. After all, he was very, very old.

The ducks, meanwhile, continued to fly on, sad at the loss of their friend. "He didn't want to die alone," said the first duck. "But it seemed to have been fated."

And the ducks flew on to their new home, with the memory of their friend with them.

# The Tiger, the Brahmin and the Jackal

## (INDIA)

The Panchatantra is a collection of animal fables recorded in verse and prose many, many, many years ago, around 200 BCE. But it's likely that the stories told in the Panchatantra are much older than that, having been part of an oral tradition.

This story, about a tiger, a Brahmin (a wise man) and a jackal, is a story about cunning and honesty. The jackal, a wolf-like animal, turns up in a lot of stories, thanks to his cleverness and his occasionally sly nature.

Once upon a time, there was a village on the outskirts of a jungle where the people had lived in peace for many years. The villagers farmed the land, growing crops and rearing livestock, selling meat, vegetables and fruit at nearby markets. Their lives were calm and filled with certainty.

Until one day, when a tiger arrived on the outskirts of the land, and the villagers' peaceful lives became full of fear. He was a large tiger, but despite his size, he moved smoothly and quietly, meaning he could surprise his prey easily. Flashes of his sharp teeth could be caught when the tiger smiled, although his smile wasn't exactly a friendly one.

The tiger would growl at the villagers and make to chase them, causing them to hide in their homes constantly. And with the villagers hiding, the tiger set about eating their animals, returning to the jungle after each feast to sleep. The tiger began by targeting the cows which the villagers used for milk. Once it had eaten all the cows, it moved on to the sheep and goats, meaning the villagers did not have meat to eat or to sell at the market. And then, the tiger even began to hunt the chickens that laid eggs for the villagers.

"What are we to do?" asked one of the villagers upon seeing only feathers where there used to be chickens when she stepped out of her house one morning. "This tiger needs to be stopped."

With hardly any animals left, the villagers were running out of food and they were terrified that the tiger would begin to see them as his next meal. So they gathered one afternoon – safe in the knowledge that the tiger had gone into the jungle for a long nap because he'd eaten another batch of chickens – in the centre of the village to try and hatch a plan.

"Perhaps we can strike a deal with the tiger," suggested one old man. "If we offer him something he really wants, then he might go away."

"What would we offer him?" said the woman who used to own lots of chickens. "We have nothing left; he's eaten it all! And we can't trust that he'll keep to his word."

There was more discussion and more suggestions were thrown out and then discarded. *What if I fight the tiger? What if we trick him? What if we scare him away?*

Finally, quiet fell over the group, and it was at this moment that one of the village elders, an old and wise woman who had been listening carefully, spoke up. "Everything that has been suggested is too difficult, or too foolish, or relies on the tiger being honourable," she said. "We need to go with something simple, and what is simpler than a hole in the ground and a trap?"

The villagers all bent close to listen as the elder outlined her plan. Later, in the dark of night, after making sure the tiger was not around, a group of them snuck out of their homes to dig a pit in which to trap the animal. They decided to dig the pit in the leaf-strewn wide path leading through the jungle to the village, which the tiger stalked down every day. The pit was wide and deep, and when they were done, the villagers covered it carefully with branches and leaves, making it look like its surroundings. Then, they strung a net from the trees up above which would be triggered when the tiger fell in the hole, and returned home to their beds, secure in the knowledge that the tiger would hound them no more.

The next day, the tiger approached the village again, looking forward to a tasty snack of a few chickens, followed by a main course of goat. But as he prowled down his usual path through the jungle to the village, covered in thick fallen branches, rocks and plenty of leaves and small plants, he failed to notice the big hole ahead of him, and before he knew it, he'd fallen in. A net fell from the trees above on to the top of the hole, and the tiger was trapped.

The tiger growled and roared and cursed, and tried to climb up the slippery sides of the pit, but it was too deep and he kept falling back. He couldn't even reach the net the villagers had thrown over the pit, but they were taking no chances, just in case the tiger did manage to climb up. His noise drew the village elders, who stood over the hole, peering in. Behind them gathered the villagers, laughing and clapping at their success.

"You're trapped now, and your days of frightening us are over," one of the village elders said, a content smile on her face. "No one will free you knowing that you will attack them if they do."

She walked away to join the cheering villagers, and it certainly seemed that her words were true. A few days passed, and although lots of villagers walked past on their way to and from the market and lots of the jungle's animals passed on their way to get food and water, none listened to the tiger's pleas to free him. Most of those that passed barely even stopped to listen.

That all changed when a Brahmin, passing through on his way to visit some family in a far off village, walked past.

"O wise man," called the tiger, "won't you please free me from my prison?"

The tiger sounded so pitiful that the Brahmin stopped where he was. He peered down into the hole. "How did you get trapped, Tiger?" he asked.

"I was taking my daily stroll on my way to get water from the river," said the tiger, "when I fell into this hole. Please, won't you help me out of here?"

The Brahmin considered the question. He knew it was in the tiger's nature to want to hunt and eat him, but he also heard the tiredness and pain in the tiger's voice. He thought for a long moment.

"I cannot release you, Tiger," the Brahmin said. "I know you want to be free, but as soon as I let you go, you will leap upon me and eat me."

"No!" shouted the tiger. "I would never do that to someone who shows such kindness to me. I am a powerful beast, and with that power I am loyal to those who help me. It is only those who are against me that I have a problem with."

The Brahmin considered again, but once more

shook his head and started to walk away. The tiger could see he was wavering, so he put on his silkiest and softest voice and said: "You are a clever and intelligent man. You know it is unfair to trap me in this way, and you know I should be free. I promise, if you free me, I will not eat you."

The Brahmin thought for a second more. "I believe you," he told the tiger. "You have promised not to eat me, and I know a promise is not something I would undertake lightly, and I am sure you are the same. I will free you."

The Brahmin carefully set about removing the net, tossing it behind him, and then reached out a hand for the tiger. The tiger carefully grasped it, and with some pulling and pushing, he found himself on the path again.

The Brahmin stepped back. "You are free n— oomph," the Brahmin's sentence was interrupted as the tiger leaped on him. The Brahmin landed on his back with the tiger's growling face looking down at him. The Brahmin could see the tiger's sharp claws out of the corner of his eye, and when the tiger opened his mouth to growl again, the Brahmin saw drool gathering at the corners of his lips and, even more scarily, a set of very sharp teeth that looked like they could pierce through the toughest of materials with little effort. And, well, the Brahmin was all skin and bones and meat, and not very tough to eat, he didn't think.

"Mmm," said the tiger, licking his lips. "I had nothing to eat in that trap, and I'm hungry now. You look like a good snack, Brahmin."

"But you promised not to eat me," the Brahmin stuttered out. "You promised."

"More fool you, Brahmin," said the tiger. "You are supposed to be a wise man, so you should know it's in my nature to eat people. But I should have guessed that I could trick you when you believed my story about falling into this hole. It was the villagers who trapped me, and now that I'm free, I'm going to eat you then head to the village."

The tiger bent his head to take a big bite out of the Brahmin, but before he could, the Brahmin yelled out: "STOP!"

The tiger paused. He was hungry, but he was willing to listen to what the Brahmin wanted to say. Before he ate him, of course.

The Brahmin took the chance to speak. "Let's strike a deal. We will ask the first three things we see whether you should eat me, and if they all agree, then I will peacefully lie down and let you devour me. But if one of them disagrees, you will let me go free."

The tiger was impatient, but he knew that the Brahmin would be even tastier if he ate him after waiting a little longer. "OK, Brahmin," said the tiger. "I agree."

The tiger let the Brahmin up and moved back a few paces. After the Brahmin had shaken his clothing free of leaves and dirt, the pair walked a little way down the path, where they encountered a tree. The tree was so tall that neither the Brahmin nor the tiger could see the top from where they stood, and it was covered almost entirely in rich green leaves. But there were a few areas where it looked like branches had been cut off the tree, and there were carvings in its trunk.

"O Tree," called the Brahmin, "Tiger wants to eat me; do you think he should be allowed?"

The tree rustled its leaves, and then in its slow and deep voice said: "I give humans shelter under my leaves. I give humans food from the fruit that I grow. And yet, they rip my branches apart to burn, and they carve into my trunk. Humans are ungrateful, and deserve to be eaten."

Disappointed, the Brahmin turned away, but knowing he still had two more chances, he remained optimistic. He and the tiger walked a little further along the path, until they met a buffalo. The buffalo was a large animal, clearly magnificent in his day, but now looking a little tired.

"O Buffalo," said the Brahmin, "Tiger wants to eat me; do you think he should be allowed?"

The buffalo raised his head so they could see his sad eyes. "The humans used to treat me well," he said. "When I gave them milk, they gave me fresh grass to eat and a shelter. But as soon as I got old, they turned me out and sent me to fend for myself. Humans are selfish, and deserve to be eaten."

A smirk took over the tiger's face at the buffalo's words, while the Brahmin began to feel more despondent. But he still had one more chance. He and the tiger turned back the way they had come, and soon a jackal crossed their path.

"O Jackal," said the Brahmin, "Tiger wants to eat me; do you think he should be allowed?"

The jackal was puzzled. "If Tiger wants to eat you, why doesn't he just do so?" he said. "Why are you asking me?"

And so the tiger and the Brahmin explained

what had happened, about how the tiger had been trapped in a hole and the Brahmin had been freed on the promise that the tiger wouldn't eat him.

"So let me get this straight," said the jackal, "you were trapped in a hole, Brahmin, and Tiger walked by and freed you?"

"No, no, no," said the tiger. "I was trapped in the hole by the villagers, and the Brahmin freed me."

"Oh!" said the jackal. "So the villagers trapped the Brahmin and you in a hole together?"

"No, no, no," said the tiger. "I was the one who fell in a hole dug by the villagers, and the Brahmin freed me."

"Oh!" said the jackal. "I understand completely. You were trapped in a hole, Tiger, and you leaped out and met the Brahmin in the village."

"No, no, no," shouted the tiger, growing frustrated. "You are being silly! Look, we are not far from the hole, let's go there and we can show you the trap."

So the tiger, the Brahmin and the jackal walked a little way down the path to the trap. There, the jackal picked up the net the Brahmin had cast aside. "So this is the net that the villagers used to help you climb out of the hole, Tiger?" asked the jackal.

"NO, NO, NO!" shouted the tiger. "You are being silly. This is what happened."

And with that, the tiger leaped back into the hole. "See," he called up. "I was down here, and the net you're holding, Jackal, was over the hole, so I couldn't get out. And then the Brahmin walked past and freed me."

"Like this?" asked the jackal. And before the tiger could blink, the jackal threw the net over the hole, and bound it in place.

"Yes, exactly like that," said the tiger. "Now free me so we can get your decision and I can eat the Brahmin. I'm hungry."

The jackal looked at the Brahmin and smirked. "No, I don't think we will free you," said the jackal. "If we do, you'll not just eat the Brahmin, you'll eat me too."

"But, but..." said the tiger.

"No buts," said the Brahmin. "You broke your promise last time, and I am wise enough to know that you'll break it again, Tiger."

And with that, he and the jackal walked away, leaving the dishonest tiger in his trap, still hungry.

# Four Harmonious Friends

## (Bhutan)

This parable is one of the Jataka Tales, which are part of Buddhist mythology. It is considered one of the national folktales of Bhutan and is a story that is often depicted in Bhutanese art; the four animals of the story are often shown gathered around a fruit tree.

It's also known as "Four Harmonious Animals", or "Four Harmonious Brothers". While it's a very short story, it has a very clear message about respecting each other, and especially your elders.

Once upon a time, there were four friends who lived near a fruit tree: an elephant, a monkey, a rabbit and a bird. They had met many years before, all attracted to the place because it was near a beautiful lake and had plenty of trees for food and shelter nearby.

They lived mostly in peace, although occasionally small arguments broke out. Sometimes they argued about whose turn it was to fetch water, or who was responsible for tidying up. Whenever they argued about anything, the elephant liked to claim that he should win, because he was the biggest. The monkey said he should win because he was the most acrobatic. The rabbit said he should win because he was the cheeriest, while the bird liked to declare herself the winner because she could fly.

One day, the four friends became curious as to who was the oldest among them, so they decided to measure their age by the fruit tree that grew near their homes. The tree was magnificent. It was tall and broad, with leaves that turned different colours in different seasons. And each summer, it offered up an abundance of delicious fruit that everyone loved eating.

The elephant went first. "The tree was fully

grown when I was young," he declared. "It reached into the sky, and as a young elephant my trunk could barely reach the lowest-hanging fruit."

The monkey went next: "When I was a child, this tree was also small. We grew up together. As it grew taller, I grew more able to jump higher and higher into its branches."

It was now the rabbit's turn. "This tree was a sapling when I was a baby rabbit," he said. "We were both nurtured and looked after to help us grow."

Finally, it was the bird's turn. "I ate the seeds of a nearby tree," she said, "and then I flew here and excreted the seed which grew this tree."

The animals all turned to the bird, and acknowledged her as the oldest, with the rabbit next, then the monkey, and the youngest being the elephant.

From then on, when the four friends argued, they turned to the oldest member, the bird, to settle their disagreements.

# Ordinary People

This group of stories is about regular people like you, your family and your friends. But the adventures they go on are probably a little more exciting, and not always in a good way, to the adventures we have in our lives!

# Dhon Cholecha

## (NEPAL)

*This is a well-known children's story from Newar society, inhabitants of the Kathmandu Valley. It shares some similarities with the Western tale "Cinderella" — a cruel stepmother, an absent father, a girl treated like a servant in her own home — but it's quite different.*

Once upon a time, there lived a little girl called Punthaku. She lived with her mum and her dad in a beautiful home on the edge of the forest. Also living with them was a faithful goat called Dhon Cholecha. The goat provided them with milk for many years, and she was also a companion for Punthaku.

But one day, when Punthaku was still very young, her mum fell ill, and she never got better. Months after she had died, Punthaku's dad married again, and the woman and her young daughter – just a year younger than Punthaku – came to live in their beautiful home.

Now, Punthaku's dad was a very busy man. He was often away on business for long periods of time, so he left the running of his home to his new wife. And he trusted her to bring up Punthaku like she was her own daughter.

But Punthaku's stepmother was not a kind woman, and she was cruel to Punthaku. She made her wash and clean and cook all day long. And she made her look after Dhon Cholecha, who by that time was quite old and didn't really do a whole lot apart from eat and sleep. *Really*, the stepmother thought, *I should get rid of the goat, but that would be a lot of work for me. Better to just foist her on Punthaku for the moment.*

To add to this, Punthaku's stepmother barely gave her any food – she got to have the leftovers after her stepmother and stepsister had eaten, and those were often meagre. And yet, despite her sparse diet, Punthaku looked hearty and healthy, and she had plenty of energy. This annoyed the stepmother, who was convinced that there was something else going on. Was Punthaku stealing food? If she was, the stepmother would make sure to punish her greatly.

But first, she needed proof. So she enlisted her daughter, who she'd taught by example to be cruel to Punthaku as well. "Follow Punthaku as she does her jobs," the stepmother told her daughter. "Make sure not to lose sight of her, and tell me everything about her day, especially where she gets all the food that keeps her looking so healthy."

So the next day Punthaku's stepsister followed her at a distance, watching as she scrubbed the floors and baked bread and washed clothes. During that time, all Punthaku did was work – there was no sign of her consuming anything more than a few sips of water.

After she'd completed all her household chores, Punthaku put on her cloak and shoes in preparation to do her favourite job: take the nanny goat out to pasture. "Come on, Dhon Cholecha," she said, leading her to a green meadow with plenty of lush grass to feed on.

Punthaku's stepsister followed at a distance, and when she saw Punthaku and Dhon Cholecha arrive at the grassy meadow, she hid behind a tree to watch. And there, she saw something quite extraordinary!

After eating for a little while, Dhon Cholecha approached Punthaku, who had spread her cloak on the ground and settled down. And as the stepsister watched, Dhon Cholecha opened her mouth and out came a stream of food: bread, cheese, a hunk of meat and a glass of water. Everything looked as if it had been served fresh from the kitchens.

The stepsister was mystified, and sure she was seeing things. When her mother asked her that night what had happened, the stepsister said: "I need to follow Punthaku again tomorrow, and get a better view of what happened. Then I will tell you."

The stepmother was impatient, but knew it was better to wait to get the proof she needed so she could punish Punthaku properly.

The next day, the stepsister got ready to follow Punthaku again. This time, instead of watching her while she did all her household chores, the stepsister made her way to the meadow early and hid behind a tree on the other side, so she could get a different view.

And once again, after Dhon Cholecha had eaten some luscious green grass, she walked over to Punthaku, opened her mouth and out came food that looked like it had been prepared for a palace!

The stepsister ran home. "Mother, mother!" she cried. Her mother ran out and the daughter immediately started explaining what she had seen.

"Why," said the woman, after she'd heard about Dhon Cholecha and Punthaku, "I knew there was something suspicious going on. That girl has been cheating us for months now, and I know just what to do to punish her."

When Punthaku arrived home, her stepmother called for her. "Punthaku," she said, with a cruel twist to her lips. Punthaku knew that what was coming next from her stepmother's mouth wouldn't be good. "Dhon Cholecha is old now – she doesn't provide us with any milk, and it takes more effort to look after her than she's worth. Tomorrow, we will slaughter her."

Punthaku was stunned. "What?" she said, tears springing immediately to her eyes. "No! She might not produce milk, but she keeps the meadow clean, and she doesn't cause you any trouble. Please, I will look after her in my spare time. Please don't kill her."

But Punthaku's stepmother was not to be moved, and the more Punthaku pleaded and cried, the firmer the stepmother's resolve.

Crying, Punthaku left her stepmother and headed straight for Dhon Cholecha's barn. There, between tears and hiccups, she told Dhon Cholecha what was going to happen.

"You must run away," said Punthaku. "That's the only way you'll be safe."

Dhon Cholecha was an old and very wise goat. She had watched Punthaku grow up and loved her very much, and she knew that if she ran away, Punthaku would be punished. She also knew that she was no longer strong enough to run very far or very fast.

"There, there, child," said Dhon Cholecha. "Dry your tears. I am happy to face my fate, but you must listen to me carefully, OK?"

At the stern question, Punthaku looked up, drying her tears.

Dhon Cholecha continued: "Tomorrow, after I have been slaughtered, you must gather my bones together and bury them at the end of your garden. Do this, and a fig tree will grow rapidly, with fruit you can eat to keep you well fed."

Punthaku tearfully agreed, and then embraced Dhon Cholecha for a long time, until the nanny goat pulled away and told her to go to bed. At the door of the barn, Punthaku looked back one last time at her beloved goat, knowing she'd never see her alive again.

The next day, Punthaku stayed hidden in her room, crying her eyes out at the fate that was befalling Dhon Cholecha. Her stepmother, for once, decided not to tell her off for not doing her chores, happy that she was suffering.

When night fell, Punthaku dried her tears and followed Dhon Cholecha's instructions. She gathered the nanny goat's bones and dug a hole at the end of the garden. There, she buried them and then went to bed.

The next morning, a great fig tree had sprung up where Punthaku had buried the bones, just as Dhon Cholecha had said it would. Each day, after she had finished her chores, Punthaku would climb up into the tree and feast on figs, reliving memories of her time with Dhon Cholecha.

One day, as Punthaku sat high up in the tree, an old couple approached. "O little girl," called the woman, who had a wrinkly face and was bent over a walking stick, just like the man with her. "We are hungry, would you spare us a fig or two?"

Punthaku was a kind-hearted girl, and she picked two of the juiciest-looking, biggest figs she could find and threw them down to the couple. But the old man and old woman missed them, and they fell on the floor.

"O little girl," croaked the old woman. "We are not fast enough to catch the figs you threw us, and our eyesight is not good enough to find them on the floor. Will you help us?"

Of course, Punthaku agreed. She climbed down the tree carefully, and on reaching the bottom went to pick up the figs she had thrown down. But before she could move, the old man grabbed Punthaku and began running, his wife following behind.

They were no longer stooping over, and they had abandoned their walking sticks. Their faces had smoothed out, the wrinkles no longer visible, and their cackling was full-throated instead of croaky.

Their teeth were prominent, and Punthaku could see that they were even sharper than the knives she used when she was cooking, sharper than anything human. Their hair and eyebrows were long and deep red, and almost looked like they were made of flames. Punthaku was frightened, but she kept calm, knowing crying and screaming would not bring anyone to her rescue.

Soon, the couple stopped running. Punthaku looked up when the old man put her down, and found herself standing in front of a pretty cottage. The old woman pulled her inside, and Punthaku caught a glimpse of jewels on the mantelpiece and a cupboard full of golden goblets as she was dragged into the kitchen.

The old woman tossed Punthaku inside. "We are hungry and want flatbreads for our dinner," she said to Punthaku. "Everything you need to prepare them is in here. When we come back, we expect to find everything ready."

And with that, the old woman left, and Punthaku heard the front door slamming.

She sighed and began to explore the kitchen, finding the flour and salt and water, and a pan. Once she had made the dough, Punthaku began to cook the flatbreads. It was at this point she heard a squeak, and after looking around the room to track down where the noise was coming from, she spotted a mouse peeking out at her from the doorway to its home in the wall.

"Do you want to know a secret?" asked the mouse in its squeaky voice. Punthaku nodded and awaited more from the mouse. "If you give me a piece of flatbread, then I will tell you."

Punthaku had just pulled a freshly made flatbread from the pan, and she tossed it at the mouse, who took it between his teeth and disappeared into his home. A few moments later, the mouse returned and once again he asked Punthaku the same question. She gave him another piece of flatbread, and he disappeared into his home again.

The third time he appeared, Punthaku threw him a piece of flatbread before he'd even asked his question. This time, the mouse stayed where he was and began speaking. "The old couple who live in this house are no ordinary couple," he said. "They are Lakheys, demons, and they plan to eat you."

Punthaku was horrified. Was she making flatbreads so the Lakheys could eat her with them?

The mouse continued speaking. "Pack as much gold and silver as you can, quickly," he said. "Then, before leaving, spit on each step of the staircase and leave a piece of coal on each stair as well. Lock the front door from the inside, and leave from the window."

Punthaku followed the mouse's instructions, quickly packing a bag full of jewels and more. Then she spat and put a piece of coal on each step. She locked the front door, and then slipped out of the window, running through the forest as quickly and quietly as she could.

When the Lakheys returned, they found the locked front door. Calling through it, they said: "O, little girl, will you let us in?"

The spit and the charcoal replied "yes", but nothing happened, so the Lakheys called again and again, getting the same answer each time. Growing suspicious, they broke down the front door to discover the empty cottage.

Meanwhile, Punthaku had made it back home, and seeing the jewels and treasures she had with her astonished her stepmother and stepsister. The stepmother demanded Punthaku tell her how she had come into possession of such wealth, and upon hearing the story, decided she wanted more jewels and gold, because as well as being mean she was also greedy.

The next day, the stepmother sent *her* daughter to the fig tree where, sure enough, the Lakheys appeared and kidnapped her. They took her to their cottage and ordered her to make flatbread, and then left her there.

But, when the mouse appeared, the stepsister refused to give it any flatbread. She refused again the second time the mouse asked. The third time, she threw a hot poker at the mouse, who ran away into his home.

And so, because she hadn't been kind to the mouse, she didn't get the instructions about gathering the jewels, leaving the coal and running away. And so, she was still there when the Lakheys returned, hungry...

When the daughter didn't arrive home that evening, the stepmother began to worry and went off in search of her daughter. She walked through the forest and eventually found the Lakheys' cottage and banged on the door. The old woman answered and, still hungry, pulled her inside and proceeded to have a second dinner.

And Punthaku, with her jewels and wealth and, most importantly, her kindness towards others, lived a happy and healthy life.

# No Time for Waiting

## (Bangladesh)

This story begins a little like "The Princess and the Salt", but it then goes in a very different direction!

It plays on the word "sobur", which means "wait", and can also mean "patience".

This is from Folk-Tales of Bengal by Lal Behari Dey, and was originally called "The Story of Prince Sobur". Behari Day was an Indian writer and journalist, who converted to Christianity, and then became a Christian missionary himself.

There was once a rich merchant with seven daughters who wanted for nothing. One day, he asked them by whose fortune they got their living.

"By you, Father," the oldest replied. The next five daughters all said the same, and the merchant was pleased as he turned to his youngest daughter, expecting to hear the same thing from her.

"I get my living by my own fortune," said the youngest daughter. Aashi, for that was her name, was just fourteen years old, so her father, at first, thought maybe she had misunderstood the question due to her youthfulness.

"By whose fortune do you get your living?" he asked again.

Aashi's answer remained the same: "By my own fortune."

The merchant was incensed, and called for his servants. "This ungrateful girl is no longer a daughter of mine," he said. "Get a palki and take her far away from here and leave her. She is not welcome in this home any more."

Aashi was whisked away by the servants, but before she left she persuaded them to let her grab her needles and thread. And then she was outside the house, about to clamber into the palki.

"Wait!"

Aashi turned around at the shout and found her old nurse running over to her. "I am going with her," the nurse told the servants. They shrugged and helped the woman climb into the palki alongside Aashi, and then they were off.

The palki bearers walked for hours and hours and hours. As the sun began to go down, they arrived at the edge of the forest, where they left Aashi and her nurse. The forest was dark and dense, and Aashi and the nurse soon found themselves standing in front of a giant tree by a stream, too afraid to go any further and wondering what fate would befall them once it got completely dark.

Seeing them looking terrified, the tree they stood by spoke. "There are many animals in this forest that would try to attack you in the dark," it said in a low yet booming voice. "You may take shelter from them all in my trunk tonight."

As Aashi and the nurse watched, the giant tree's trunk split down the middle, revealing a space in which the pair could both sit comfortably. They climbed inside and the tree sealed back up.

Dark fell, and the hunters of the forest began their hunt for prey. Soon, they could smell the enticing scents of humans, and they followed the trail to the tree. There, the smell was strongest and the animals – tigers and wolves and jackals – began attacking the tree in turn, trying to get inside. They scratched and bit and clawed at the tree trunk, chipping away bits of wood. But, as much as they tried, they could not get inside.

Soon, the sun began to rise and, defeated, the animals slunk off to their homes.

Once it was fully light, the tree opened its trunk and out stepped Aashi and her nurse. "Oh," cried Aashi, seeing the damage that had been caused to the tree. "That must hurt."

In response, the tree simply groaned in pain.

Aashi quickly moved to the nearby stream, where she gathered mud from the banks to coat the tree's wounds.

"Thank you," said the tree. "That feels much better. But now, I can hear you are both hungry."

Aashi and the nurse looked at each other – their stomachs *had* been rumbling.

"Nurse, take what money you have and go to the nearby town," the tree instructed. "There, buy as much khai as you can and bring it back here."

The nurse and Aashi emptied out their pockets,

and between them found a few pitiful coins, but nowhere near enough for the rice snack the tree had instructed them to buy. But the tree had looked after them well until now and so they agreed to trust it.

The nurse went off to the town and found a khai seller. But when she showed her money, the seller laughed at her. "You can't get any khai for that," she scoffed. "Get away from here."

A little dejected, the nurse moved to the next stall, where the seller had seen what had happened. She felt sorry for the nurse, and gave her a generous amount of khai, even though the nurse didn't have much money.

When she returned to Aashi and the tree, the nurse showed them the khai. "Take half and eat it," said the tree. "Take the other half, and scatter it along the bank of the stream in front of me."

Puzzled, the pair nevertheless followed the tree's instructions. That night, they crept back into the tree to sleep, while once again the animals tried to get in.

When they woke up the next morning and stepped outside, they were greeted with an astonishing sight: hundreds of peacocks were on the bank of the river in front of the tree, eating the khai the nurse had scattered there. When they were finished, they wandered off, but in their wake left dozens of beautiful peacock feathers.

Aashi and the nurse gathered the feathers together and, using the needles and thread she had managed to bring from home, Aashi made a beautiful fan. The nurse took the fan into town, where a rich merchant purchased it from her for a huge sum of money. With some of the money, the nurse bought more khai and some other food.

She and Aashi scattered the khai on the bank of the river, and ate the other food. They did this every day, and every day more peacocks came and left beautiful feathers, which Aashi made into fans of all sizes, and which the nurse sold.

Soon, the pair had saved quite a bit of money. "It is time," said the tree, "for you to build your own house. There is a clearing not far from here that will be the perfect spot."

And so Aashi and the nurse hired builders and a beautiful house was built, close enough that they could still gather peacock feathers and visit the tree on a regular basis.

*

Months and years passed, and Aashi and the nurse lived a comfortable life, never wanting for anything. They continued to expand their business and work hard, saving some money in case they had need of it in the future.

But time and fortune had not been so kind to Aashi's family. In their town, far away, the merchant had had a run of bad luck, and lost his business and then his home. With his six daughters and his wife, he was forced to move far, far away to another town. There, they lived in a tiny house and tried to scrape a living doing odd jobs.

Now, it just so happened that this town was the one closest to Aashi and the nurse. One day, the merchant and his wife heard that there was a local businesswoman who was in need of some household help, so they decided to make their way into the forest to see if they could get jobs.

As they walked up the path to the house, Aashi was looking out of the window. Despite their bedraggled appearance, their old clothes and their tired faces, Aashi immediately recognized them as her parents and, even though she had been thrown out of their house, she still loved them deeply.

The couple were greeted at the door by servants,

who took them into a grand room, where beautiful clothes were laid out. The merchant and his wife were told to get changed into the grand clothing, and then the servants left them.

Confused and too afraid to disobey, the pair did as they were told. What was happening? Were they to be entertainment for the rich woman who owned the house? Would they be mocked and laughed at?

Then the doors opened and in walked Aashi. Many years had passed, and she was no longer the girl her parents had last seen, so they didn't recognize her at first, although both secretly felt there was something about her that was familiar.

Aashi didn't hesitate. "Mother, Father, it is me, Aashi," she said, holding out her arms to them both. Her mother and father rushed into her embrace.

"Daughter, forgive me," said her father, sobbing.

"All is forgiven, Father," said Aashi. "Come, sit with me and we can tell each other everything about our lives."

And so the merchant and his wife shared how they had fallen on hard times, and Aashi told them about her life and how she had made her living.

"You were right, daughter," said the merchant. "You do live by your own fortune, and not mine."

Later that day, Aashi was reunited with her sisters, who were all astonished – and a little bit jealous – to see the wealth that their youngest sibling had gathered over the years. They didn't say anything out loud, but all stewed on the inside, even as Aashi generously gave them new clothes and fed them a feast like they hadn't had in years.

To her father, Aashi gave money to help him restart his business as a merchant. With the money, the merchant hired a ship to take him to faraway places, where he would buy and sell goods. But on the day the ship was due to leave, it wouldn't move. The merchant pondered over this problem and then realized: he had asked all his daughters except Aashi what they would like him to bring back from his voyage.

The merchant sent a messenger to Aashi's house. When the messenger arrived and asked Aashi what she wanted, she was in the middle of doing something, and said to the messenger: "Sobur." Misunderstanding her instruction to wait, the messenger headed back to the ship, and told the merchant that Aashi wanted him to bring back Sobur for her.

The merchant set off, and visited many places on

his trip: large cities, small villages, quiet towns and bustling ports. He quickly gathered the jewellery and clothing and spices his six oldest daughters had requested, but in every town he asked, there was no sign of Sobur.

At his last stop, the merchant was desperate to find the gift his youngest daughter, who had been so kind to him, had requested. "Sobur," he shouted as he walked around. "I am looking for Sobur. Has anyone seen Sobur?"

Suddenly, he was stopped by a young man who was accompanied by a retinue of servants. "I am Prince Sobur," he said, introducing himself. "You have been shouting for me."

The merchant hadn't expected Sobur to be a person, let alone a prince, but he explained his dilemma to the man, who listened patiently.

"I have just the thing," said the prince. He gestured to one of his servants, who handed him a box. "Take this and give it to your daughter. It contains a magical fan with a looking glass, and it will fulfil her request to you."

The merchant gratefully received the box, and when he returned home from his voyage, he handed it over to Aashi. Busy organizing a feast to welcome her father home, she set it aside, planning to look at it later.

She forgot about the box, so was surprised when she came across it a few days later. This time she opened it and took out the fan inside. When she shook it open, there was a crack, and Prince Sobur appeared before her. He introduced himself and explained how he had met her father, a story which amused Aashi when she figured out the messenger's misunderstanding.

Aashi invited Prince Sobur to be her guest for as long as he wanted. He was eager to see a new kingdom and accepted, sending word for his servants to join him. During the weeks that followed, Aashi and Prince Sobur got to know one another and fell in love, and soon decided they would be married.

The celebrations approached quickly, but not everyone was happy. Aashi's older sisters, already a little jealous of her wealth and her independence, became more jealous because of her love for the handsome prince, and his for her.

And so, on the wedding day they crushed a dozen bottles into a fine powder and scattered it on to Prince Sobur's bed. The powder was so fine that it couldn't be seen, and Prince Sobur was completely unaware there was anything wrong when he lay down. But after just a few moments, the powder had made its way through his skin and he was in agony. He began shouting and moaning, tears streaming down his face. His servants, seeing his distress, magically whisked him away to his own country, where his parents – the king and queen – sent out for every healer they knew. Although they tried many different things, none of them could help and the prince remained in agony.

Back in the other kingdom, Aashi was in despair over the hurt that had been done to her husband, and was determined to go after him. She disguised herself as a soldier, and took a sword with her for the journey, which was going to be long: it would take her weeks, at the very least, to get to Prince Sobur's kingdom.

On the first day, Aashi, not used to walking so much and certainly not in the heavy clothes of a man, got tired quickly. She settled down for a nap under a tree, and soon began to doze.

The tree, unbeknown to Aashi, contained the nest of the divine bird Bihangama and his partner

Bihangami. The birds were currently out gathering food, but they had left their babies in the nest. Ordinarily, the babies would have been safe, but today a giant snake was nearby and was determined to get at the nest and have a tasty meal.

The snake slowly slithered up the side of the tree, and when the baby birds saw it they began squawking loudly and crying. Their noise woke Aashi from her nap. When she glanced to the side and saw the snake, she leaped into action, grabbing her sword and, without thinking, slashing the snake in two, saving the birds.

The Bihangama and Bihangami had been returning to the nest and had also heard the noises from their babies. As they flew back, they worried that they were too late, and the snake would have eaten their children.

But when they returned, they saw Aashi standing over the snake, and their babies safe in their nest.

"We must thank this soldier for his bravery and his quick thinking," said the Bihangami to the Bihangama.

"Ah, this is no man," said the Bihangama who, being a divine bird, knew lots of things others did not. "This soldier is a woman, and her name is

Aashi. She was married recently and her husband was attacked. She is on her way to try and save him."

And the Bihangama told his partner what had happened, and how none of the humans could work out a cure for what had befallen Prince Sobur.

"No cure?" said the Bihangami in dismay.

The Bihangami's voice, which had increased in volume in her upset, caused Aashi to look up. She bowed when she saw the pair, knowing their status.

"No, no," said the Bihangami. "You have saved our children. There is no need to bow to us. I only wish there was something we could do to help you in return, but I understand there is no cure for what ails your husband."

"There is a cure," said the Bihangama, surprising his partner and Aashi, who looked at him hopefully. Turning to Aashi, he continued: "Take our droppings and grind them into a fine powder. Then apply it to the prince with a brush after bathing him seven times with seven jars of water and seven jars of milk."

Aashi gathered the droppings and began grinding them into a fine powder.

As she did this, the Bihangami turned to the

Bihangama: "It will take Aashi weeks, if not more, to travel to Prince Sobur, and by that point, it may be too late. Is there any way we can get her there quicker?"

"I will take her on my back, and she will be there in a flash," said the Bihangama. And so, when Aashi was ready, the powder stored in a small jar, she climbed on the Bihangama's back, and he soared into the air. With a speed unlike any she had ever seen or heard of, the Bihangama transported her to Prince Sobur's kingdom, and the doors of the palace.

There, Aashi, still dressed as a soldier, petitioned to be allowed to treat Prince Sobur. By this time, the king and queen had almost lost hope. They didn't believe there was anything that could make their son well again, but they didn't think there was any harm in letting the soldier who had turned up at their door try.

Aashi made her way to Prince Sobur's room, where she called for the milk and water the Bihangama had told her about. She bathed the prince seven times with seven jars of milk and seven jars of water, and brushed him with the powder.

As she came to the end, the prince stirred, and the pained expression on his face disappeared. He slowly woke, still disorientated, and saw the delighted faces of his parents peering over him and a figure, a soldier, standing in the background. After speaking briefly with his mother and father, the prince drifted off to sleep again, for he still needed to rest and recover.

"You have saved my son," said the king to Aashi. "You have my eternal thanks, but you may also ask for anything you want as a reward. I can give you gold or jewels or land or horses. Whatever you desire."

Aashi thought for a moment. "All I ask," she said, "is for the ring from Prince Sobur's finger."

The king granted her request, and upon receiving the ring, Aashi took her leave and headed to the gates of the palace, where the Bihangama was waiting. She climbed on to its back and he transported her back home.

After a couple of days to rest, and to make sure Prince Sobur was rested, Aashi took the magical fan with the looking glass out of its box, and shook it. Immediately, Prince Sobur appeared before her and the pair embraced.

And then, Aashi held out her hand, upon which sat Prince Sobur's ring. He knew in an instant that the Sannyasi who had cured him was in fact his wife Aashi. They embraced once again, and from that moment on, no one could separate them.

# A Pot of Silver

## (AFGHANISTAN)

*This is a folktale from Afghanistan about hard work and honesty.*

Once upon a time, there was a poor farmer who worked very hard. Every day, he woke up early to tend to his crops in the fields. He returned home late every night, exhausted from a day toiling away outside, looking after the wheat and making sure it grew as tall as possible and in abundance.

But despite his hard work, he only ever made enough from his crops to buy just enough food for himself and his wife to last until he could next get to market to sell his goods. The market was a few hours away, and going there by foot to sell his crops took a whole day, and was even more tiring than looking after his farm.

Every night before bed, no matter how tired he was, the farmer prayed. And he always prayed for the same thing. "Oh, please, grant me riches in my hearth," he would say, before getting into bed and falling asleep.

One day, the farmer was out checking his fields when he caught his shirt on the fence that separated his land from his neighbour's. The fence had been broken for a while.

"I guess," he said to himself, "now is the time to fix this fence."

The farmer got his tools and began to dig around

the fence post. Once he'd removed it, he decided to make the hole a little deeper so the fence would be more secure, but as he dug, there was a loud clanging noise. The farmer had hit something that definitely wasn't soil.

Kneeling down, the farmer scraped away a layer of soil and saw a silver metal box. He loosened the soil around it until he could grab its sides, and heaved it out. The box was clearly very old and made of metal. It had flowers carved on all sides, and a lock dangling from the front, although it was not locked.

"Phew, this is heavy," said the farmer, sitting back and taking a rest. After drinking some water, the farmer wiped the box clean and then forced open the lid – he had to put some effort in because the box had not been opened in a long time and the lid was very stiff. And what did the farmer see inside? Hundreds and hundreds of silver coins! No wonder the box had been so heavy.

At first, the farmer was overjoyed because he thought his prayers had been answered. But then he remembered that he had asked for riches in his hearth. He knew that taking something that wasn't meant for him would be bad, so he secured the lid back on to the box, and buried the box where he had found it. He dug a new hole for the fence post next to its old position, and after fixing it in place, went home for the day.

When he got home, he greeted his wife, who had prepared a small dinner for them. While they ate, he told her about his discovery.

"You did what?" the farmer's wife exclaimed after hearing that the farmer had reburied the silver. "Why would you do that?"

"It was not meant for me," the farmer said. "If I'd taken it, who knows what bad things would have happened to us?"

The farmer's wife scoffed, and for the rest of the evening refused to speak to her husband. She had always been an unhappy and selfish woman, who wanted nothing more than to be rich and laze around doing nothing.

When her husband fell asleep, the farmer's wife slipped out of the house and knocked on her neighbour's door, telling him what had happened.

"The box is buried next to the fence post," she told the neighbour. "You should go and get it tonight, and we can share the riches."

The neighbour agreed and headed out to the

farmer's land with a shovel. It took him an hour to trek out to the spot, using the moon and stars to light the way, and it was quiet when he got there, the only noise the occasional hoot of a bird. He found the fence post, and saw the newly dug soil next to it. He began digging, and only stopped when he heard a clunk as his shovel hit something hard and metal.

"Aha," said the neighbour. He pulled out the box and placed it on the ground. It was very heavy, and the neighbour took a moment to rest, building up the anticipation for what he would see when he opened the box. Slowly, he opened the lid, which wasn't as stiff because it had already been opened once earlier in the day, but immediately snapped it shut again after glimpsing what was inside and, more scarily, hearing it.

"That sneaky old woman," he said. "There's no silver in here, it's just a bunch of snakes. I bet she hoped I'd stick my hand inside and be poisoned, and then she could take my home and my land. More fool her, she'll get what she deserves."

Making sure the box was completely sealed, the neighbour slowly carried it back to his house. Once there, he set the box down so he could get a ladder from his barn, which he set against the farmer's house. Then he climbed with the box up to the roof.

At the top, he held the box upside down over the chimney and quickly opened the lid, watching as the snakes fell down into the farmer's house.

"That'll teach the old woman to try and trick me," the neighbour said.

The farmer's wife had been waiting up by the hearth, thinking about all the things she would buy with her new-found wealth. The first thing she planned to do was go to the city and rent a beautiful house, and then buy some fancy clothes for herself. As she daydreamed, she heard a noise from the chimney, and watched in shock as dozens of snakes poured out on to the hearth. She leaped back, knocking over the stool she was sitting on, and ran out the front door. "I refuse to stay here any longer," she shrieked.

The next morning, the farmer woke up early as usual. He noticed that his wife, usually a late riser, was not in the cottage. He took a quick look outside, and found a note on the tree stump where he cut wood for the cottage. The farmer had to admit he wasn't surprised that his wife had left;

she had always been more suited to the city, and she would be happier there.

The farmer made his way back to the kitchen to light the hearth for breakfast, and that was when he noticed an unusual sight. Covering the ashes from the day before were coins, hundreds and hundreds and hundreds of silver coins.

"My prayers have been answered!" the farmer exclaimed. "I wanted riches in my hearth, and they have arrived."

And so, the farmer lived happily ever after, able to grow his business with the money from his hearth, hiring workers to help him and better equipment to make his job easier.

# The Merchant and the Con Man

## (PAKISTAN)

*This story appeared in* The Olive Fairy Book *by Andrew Lang.*

Once upon a time, there was a merchant called Ahmed who worked very hard. When he first started out, as a youth, he didn't make very much money, but after years of working, he found himself very wealthy. He was careful to take all the opportunities that came his way, to turn things down if they seemed too risky, and most importantly, he saved. He was careful with his money, buying all the things he needed and some of the things he wanted, but making sure to put most of his money aside.

With his new wealth, the merchant found himself longing for his ancestral home, a small and beautiful village that was many days' journey away. Knowing he could now build his own house there, he decided to return home to his family.

But Ahmed was clever and knew he couldn't journey for days with all his gold. So instead, he bought a number of small jewels with his money, and stored them in an unassuming wooden box. It was a little scuffed and looked quite unimpressive, and Ahmed knew few people would wonder what was inside. He locked the box, dressed humbly in a pair of brown trousers, a cream shirt and a brown cloak – all of which looked like they were well used – and started off on his journey.

Ahmed took a wagon out of the city, and spent two days and two nights travelling over rickety roads. The wagon, pulled by two horses, clambered over grassy fields and rough tracks, through woods and along a cliff. Other passengers got on and off the wagon when it stopped at small towns and villages, but Ahmed stayed on.

Until finally, when he was two days away from home, Ahmed decided to stop in the nearest big city to his village to buy some clothes more befitting of his wealth. He found a busy bazaar filled with noise and colour. Shopkeepers shouted about their goods – "try the best samosas you'll ever eat", "buy my tea and you'll never have a cold again" – and the delicious smells of cooking food mixed with the scents of animals and people.

Among all the shops, Ahmed spotted a clothing store, which grabbed his attention because it was quiet instead of noisy. The shopkeeper sat on the floor, drinking a cup of tea, surrounded by bolts of beautiful fabric and ready-made clothes. It was a riot of colour, every kind of red and blue and green you'd ever seen, fabrics printed with pictures that looked like paintings, and others which had patterns that made your eyes blur if you looked at them too long. There were silks and wools, satins and cottons.

Ahmed sat down opposite the shopkeeper and showed interest in a few pieces. As he spoke more, the shopkeeper, a man called Beeka Ram, began to suspect that Ahmed was richer than he appeared. He spoke about clothing and materials with the knowledge of someone who had experience with expensive fabrics, and he knew exactly what he wanted, naming some of the latest styles of cloaks and trousers when he spoke.

Beeka Ram was a cunning man, and his shop was located not just in a busy bazaar, but in the centre of all criminal activity in the city. There were thieves and con men everywhere, but Beeka Ram was the best of them all. Knowing that he could possibly get something from the merchant, he offered to let him change into his new clothes in the private room at the back of the shop.

When the merchant came back out wearing a pair of deep blue trousers, a matching kurta and a magnificent black cloak lined in a blue satin, Beeka Ram asked him where he was going.

"I am returning home to my village after many years away," said Ahmed, giving the name of the village. When Beeka Ram's face fell immediately, Ahmed asked: "What is it?"

"The road to that village is very dangerous," said Beeka Ram hesitantly. "It is full of thieves who will take every little thing you are carrying. Just last week a wealthy merchant was robbed of all his jewels and money by a gang of men who hid in the trees, waiting for him to come past. All they left him with was the kurta and trousers he was wearing; they even took his shoes and cloak!"

Ahmed became worried about his box of jewels, and having spotted a safe when he was getting changed, asked Beeka Ram if he could take care of a small box for him for a few days.

"I am just a clothing merchant," Beeka Ram replied, although secretly he was very pleased to be conning a clearly rich man. "I cannot possibly take care of anything for you."

"Please," said Ahmed. "It is just a small wooden box, and I will be back in four days to collect it. It won't take up much room at all. You'll barely notice it's there, and it won't put you in any danger. It simply contains some items that have value to me."

Beeka Ram pretended to consider Ahmed's request for a moment, and then agreed. So the merchant handed over the box, and after seeing Beeka Ram carefully place it in the safe, he left the shop.

But it felt strange to have handed over his wealth and he had seen what he thought was a strange look on the shopkeeper's face when he left. So before Ahmed departed from the bazaar, he asked the other shopkeepers about Beeka Ram. Being criminals and con men themselves, they all told Ahmed that Beeka Ram was a trustworthy man. Feeling better, Ahmed made his way out of the bazaar and to his village.

As soon as he disappeared from sight, Beeka Ram scurried into the back room of his shop, where he quickly unlocked the safe. Taking the box out, he grabbed his tools and made quick work of the box's lock. Taking a breath before he opened it, he lifted the lid and smiled widely when he saw the shiny jewels winking up at him. "Ha ha!" exclaimed Beeka Ram. "These treasures will do very nicely indeed." Closing the box, Beeka Ram put it back in the safe, and went off to imagine all that he might buy with the jewels.

Four days later, as promised, Ahmed returned to the bazaar, this time with six of his nephews – all strong young men – in tow to help him guard the box as they travelled back to the village. While his nephews wandered the city, Ahmed made his way to the bazaar. As he walked past the shopkeepers in Beeka Ram's street, they all burst into laughter one by one as they saw him.

"Hello, Beeka Ram," said Ahmed, when he reached the shop and saw the shopkeeper. But he received no answer in return. Thinking that Beeka Ram hadn't heard him over the noise and hubbub of the bazaar, Ahmed spoke louder. "Hello, Lala-ji, remember me?"

Beeka Ram looked at the merchant. "Who are you?" he asked.

Ahmed was shocked, but knew that the shopkeeper saw hundreds of people a day, and that maybe he just couldn't place where he knew Ahmed from. "I bought clothing from you four days ago, and left a small wooden box in your care," Ahmed said patiently. "I have come to retrieve the box and take it home with me."

Beeka Ram laughed out loud. "I have no idea who you are," he said, turning away from the merchant. "Please leave my shop."

Ahmed's shock turned into upset. "Please,

Lala-ji," he pleaded. "You must know who I am. I simply want to collect my box and be on my way."

Beeka Ram smirked, but changed his facial expression to one of anger as he turned back round. "I said I do not know who you are," he said sternly. "Now leave my shop, or I will have to call someone to have you removed."

"But, but," stuttered Ahmed. "We just saw each other a few days ago. I left a wooden box in your keeping, and watched you put it in the safe. Please return it to me."

"I told you to leave," shouted Beeka Ram, frightening Ahmed. The merchant didn't want to be thrown out, and knowing he was defeated, he left the shop, going round the corner and sitting by its wall. There, he cried tears for the loss of his wealth, and for being foolish enough to trust a stranger.

The day passed, and Beeka Ram, happy to have conned the merchant out of his jewels, locked up his shop and went home. Ahmed continued to sit by the wall as night fell, having sent his nephews back to the village without him, ashamed of being taken in by a con man and knowing there was nothing they could do.

Many people had walked past Ahmed and said nothing to him. They hadn't even looked at him. But one young man, walking home late at night, did notice Ahmed. The man's name was Kooshy Ram, and he was very, very rich, but as a young man he had no idea how to look after his money, and simply spent it on parties for his friends. Kooshy Ram was curious about the sad-looking merchant who seemed to be readying to sleep outside, even though he looked wealthy. But Kooshy Ram was tired and when he got home, he fell asleep quickly with no more thoughts of the merchant.

The next morning, Kooshy Ram got up for a late breakfast, and saw the merchant again, still sitting by the shop. Although Kooshy Ram was sometimes a little foolish, he was kind-hearted and went up to Ahmed.

"You have been sitting here all night," he said to him. "Do you need some help? Are you lost? Are you hungry?"

"There is no helping me," Ahmed said, his voice full of despair.

Kooshy Ram sat down opposite him. "Well, if I can't help, perhaps I can listen to your story and help lighten your burden in that way," he said.

And so Ahmed told Kooshy Ram about how he had worked hard for years, and saved his money. He told him about his journey home, and how he had stopped to buy new clothes from Beeka Ram, and then entrusted him to look after his box of jewels.

At that point, Kooshy Ram laughed out loud, causing Ahmed to become even more upset. "I am sorry for laughing," Kooshy Ram said quickly, not meaning to hurt Ahmed, "but everyone here knows that Beeka Ram is a thief and a con man."

"Everyone except me," said Ahmed sadly.

"Look," said Kooshy Ram. "I think I might be able to help you. I need to go and speak to some people, and then I will be back in a couple of days."

Kooshy Ram left, and Ahmed continued to sit round the side of Beeka Ram's shop. For two days, he spoke to no one, although he saw Kooshy Ram pass by sometimes, speaking and laughing with a couple of friends. One was very, very tall, while the other always wore a brightly coloured turban.

Two days later, Kooshy Ram returned to speak to Ahmed early in the morning. "Later today, make sure you are standing across the road from Beeka Ram's shop," he said. "When you receive a signal, you need to go and ask Beeka Ram for your box back."

"But what use will that be?" asked Ahmed. "He won't return it to me."

"Trust me," said Kooshy Ram. And so, with nothing else to lose, Ahmed agreed.

Later that day, Ahmed took up a post across the road from Beeka Ram's shop, and soon afterwards, he saw a grand palanquin being carried by four men – one at each corner – coming down the lane of the bazaar. The palanquin was a royal purple, with a small window outlined in gold carvings. The curtain pulled over the window was a matching purple. Ahmed recognized two of the men – the very, very tall one and the one with the brightly coloured turban – as being the friends he had seen with Kooshy Ram in the bazaar.

The men set the palanquin down outside Beeka Ram's shop, and the shop owner ran out immediately, recognizing the wealth of the palanquin.

The very, very tall man stepped forward. "My mistress is on a long journey, and her husband cannot travel further with her at this stage, so her guard will be reduced," said the man. "She had heard this is a safe place to leave her jewels while she completes her journey, and she can then send someone back for them."

With that, the other men who had been carrying the palanquin pulled out four boxes and opened them to show Beeka Ram. Within were reams of precious jewels and gold. There were diamond necklaces, and thick bracelets studded with rubies and emeralds, as well as gold bars. Beeka Ram's eyes grew large.

"Oh yes," he said greedily. "I can definitely store those for your mistress."

At that moment, Ahmed saw an arm slip through the purple curtain of the palanquin and start frantically waving at him. Deciding this must be the signal, he crossed over to the shop.

"Beeka Ram," said Ahmed. "I have come to collect the box you stored for me and said you would return."

Beeka Ram was displeased, but knew if he did not return the box he wouldn't look trustworthy. And while the merchant's jewels were good, he knew that the woman in the palanquin was far richer, and a much bigger con.

"Wait one moment," said Beeka Ram. And he went inside and retrieved the merchant's jewels from the safe. He was sad to part with them, but they were nothing compared to the riches that he'd been shown, belonging to the wealthy woman.

Beeka Ram stepped outside his shop and held the box out to Ahmed, who quickly grabbed it and clutched it to his chest. Part of Ahmed wanted to run away now that he had his box, but a bigger part wanted to see what would happen next, and how Kooshy Ram was involved. Ahmed watched as Beeka Ram turned back to the boxes of jewels open in front of the palanquin, but before anyone could say anything, a messenger rushed up.

"The master has decided he is able to travel with the mistress," said the messenger. "There is no need to leave the jewels here for safekeeping, as enough guards will be travelling with them now."

The boxes were quickly shut, leaving Beeka Ram shocked. In the next moment, the person in the palanquin stepped out, and it wasn't a woman but Kooshy Ram! Ahmed was overjoyed, and laughed at seeing the gobsmacked look on Beeka Ram's face at the revelation that he had been conned.

Seeing him, Ahmed began dancing in the street, and Kooshy Ram joined him. "Thank you for arranging the return of my jewels," Ahmed said.

"Thank you for trusting me," Kooshy Ram said, as the two men continued to dance, getting further and further away from the merchant's shop, the palanquin full of the treasure chests following them.

And so the two men wandered out of sight, off to become dear friends and business partners. And Beeka Ram was left humiliated, no longer the best con man in the street of thieves, and was instead mocked by all his fellow shopkeepers.

# A Ghostly Wife

## (BANGLADESH)

*This story comes from Lal Behari Dey's* Folk-Tales *from Bengal.*

Once upon a time, there lived a Brahmin. He was married, and his mother lived with him and his wife.

The Brahmin's wife, whose name was Poorna, wasn't very good at household chores. She wasn't a very good cook, and it took her for ever to tidy up. Whenever she made bread, it came out rock solid. When she made the bed, it took her all day because she always got distracted. When she washed clothes, she forgot to hang them out to dry. Now, she was very good at other things – she was an excellent writer, she could sing beautifully, she was very clever and knew four languages – but for the purposes of this story, her being bad at cooking and cleaning is relevant.

One morning, Poorna went out to collect water. She liked this chore because it meant she could walk through the woods, and come up with ideas for new things to write about. Caught up in her own world, Poorna didn't notice when she brushed by a Sakchinni, a kind of ghost, in the forest.

But the Sakchinni, who was quick to take offence and to anger, did notice. Within moments, she'd gathered up Poorna and stuffed her in a tree trunk. The Sakchinni took on Poorna's appearance and then headed back to the Brahmin and the mother-in-law. Since she looked exactly like Poorna, neither were suspicious.

However, the next morning when the mother-in-law woke up to get breakfast on, she smelled food. This was unusual because Poorna was never up this early to cook, and whenever she did cook, there was always a smell of burning drifting through the house.

Going through to the kitchen, the mother-in-law saw a breakfast feast laid out on the table. There were delicately puffed flatbreads, perfectly golden and crisp, alongside a spicy potato curry. Deep-fried egg parathas were piled high on a plate, alongside glistening chutneys. Steam could be seen curling up from a pot of richly coloured tea, and the smells of cardamom and cinnamon drifted up and around the room. Poorna was stood to one side, nudging the fire to get it to burn brighter, casting the room with warmth and a pleasant flow. The mother-in-law was stunned, but her mouth was already watering. She tucked into the spread, as did the Brahmin when he appeared.

Over the next few days, Poorna continued to cook delicious dishes. In addition, she cleaned the house so thoroughly that her mother-in-law knew something was wrong. She decided to keep a close eye on Poorna.

One day, she asked Poorna to fetch her a cup. Before the request had finished leaving her mouth, Poorna was presenting a cup to her. Later, the mother-in-law asked for a biscuit, and this time she clamped her gaze on Poorna as she made her request. To her astonishment, she saw Poorna's arm extend beyond any human's reach and then come back with a biscuit from the kitchen.

That night, the mother-in-law spoke to her son, and the pair agreed they needed to see one more instance of this suspicious behaviour. So the next day, the Brahmin asked Poorna for a clean shirt. Before his very eyes, her arms extended and she snapped it back, holding a new shirt from his room two doors away.

The Brahmin and his mother agreed that Poorna was not herself, and had been possessed by something, so they called an ojha. When the exorcist arrived, he decided to carry out a test to see if Poorna was really possessed by a ghost.

He burned some turmeric and wafted it around the house. Ghosts can't stand the smell of burning turmeric, and before a few seconds had passed, Poorna started screaming.

The ojha caught Poorna, or what they had all thought was Poorna, and after some persuasion she told them she was a Sakchinni and that she had kidnapped Poorna when the woman had bumped into her by accident.

After the Sakchinni revealed where she'd hidden Poorna, the Brahmin rushed to find her, and brought her back.

The ojha made the Sakchinni promise not to harm Poorna or the Brahmin or their family, and then let her go.

And Poorna and the Brahmin lived happily ever after (although she was still a bad cook).

# The Tale of the Gurumapa

## (Nepal)

The gurumapa is a mythical creature from the folklore of Nepal, and his story is one of the most well-known folktales from Newar society, the historical inhabitants of the Kathmandu Valley and its surrounding areas.

The gurumapa is a bit like an ogre – he's large and has a scary face, and he's often used to scare children who won't go to sleep!

Once upon a time, there was a young man called Kesh Chandra who came from a wealthy family. He was the youngest in his family, and a little spoilt because of it. He didn't have a job, and lived off the money his parents had given him to set up a business. He was bored, and instead of occupying himself with work or hobbies, he got into the habit of playing games and making wagers with friends at parties.

But soon he began making wagers with strangers as well, and eventually he ran out of money. His father, who had tried many times to advise his son, had had enough and banned Kesh Chandra from his house, telling him to make his own way. Devastated, Kesh Chandra went to his older sister, who had a successful business of her own, and threw himself on her mercy.

The sister loved Kesh Chandra, and had many memories of the pair playing games together as children and sneaking sweets from the kitchen at home. She welcomed Kesh Chandra into her home like an honoured guest, serving him a delicious meal on a plate made of gold. She had a busy day full of meetings the next day, so she went to bed, leaving her brother to eat his meal alone. Kesh

Chandra devoured the food and, on the spur of the moment, took the plate, knowing that it was worth a bit of money. That night, after spending the few pennies he had found in his clothes, he wagered the plate in a game, and lost.

The next day he went back to his sister's house, and she once more took mercy on him. This time, she gave him food on a silver plate. Once more, he ate the food and took the plate, losing it in a wager that night.

A third time, Kesh Chandra went back to his sister's house. Still patient with him, even though he had lost her gold and silver plates which she had bought with her hard-earned money, she served him food on a bronze plate because she loved him. Once more, though, after eating the food, Kesh Chandra left for the night, went to a party, wagered the plate and lost it.

The next day, when he returned to his sister's house, he found her angry. "No more," she shouted. "You have answered my love and hospitality with lying and cheating. This is the last meal I will give you." And with that, she threw his food on to the floor in front of him.

Kesh Chandra was upset and hungry, so gathered

the food in a handkerchief and left his sister's house. He wandered for hours, covering miles and miles, leaving the city and going through the woods and fields. Soon, he needed a rest and sustenance, so he sat by a tree to eat the food his sister had cooked. But when he opened the handkerchief, he saw the food had gone mouldy because it was so hot, and had maggots crawling on it.

He decided to spread it on the floor in the hope that the maggots went away and the food dried a little. The day was very warm, but under the tree where he sat it was pleasantly cool, and soon Kesh Chandra drifted off to sleep.

When he awoke, he was more than ready to eat, but to his dismay, he saw pigeons eating the last of the food. As he despaired about what he would do, he saw one of the pigeons had left droppings where the food used to be, and the droppings were made of gold! Then more pigeons started making droppings, and they were all gold too. *All this gold will surely help me make a fresh start*, thought Kesh Chandra.

Kesh Chandra gathered up the droppings, and soon there were too many for him to carry. He placed them all in a pile as he contemplated how to move the heavy load. At that moment, he heard a noise behind him.

Turning, he saw a gurumapa coming out of the woods, and it looked hungry. The tall and ogre-like gurumapa, who was at least twice the height of a human adult, lumbered towards him. The gurumapa had tough-looking hands and feet, and fangs protruding from his wide mouth. His sharp eyes bore into Kesh Chandra, and there was no doubt in the man's mind that this creature wanted to eat him.

Thinking quickly, Kesh Chandra shouted: "Stop!"

Startled, the gurumapa stopped in his tracks. Kesh Chandra hurried to speak: "You look like you are hungry, but I have been walking for a long time and I'm not tasty. If you help me to transport this gold to the next village, I promise I will have a feast made for you, and you won't go hungry again."

The gurumapa thought about it. "But I will need food every month," he growled.

"There is plenty to eat in the village," Kesh Chandra said. "You can have a meal every month."

The gurumapa agreed, and carted the gold easily on to his back, following Kesh Chandra through the fields and into the nearby village.

There, Kesh Chandra used his gold to buy a beautiful house, and he immediately arranged for a meal to be prepared, which he took to the gurumapa, who had returned to wait at the edge of the village. The gurumapa devoured the meats and breads that had been prepared for him, and then returned to his home.

Things were peaceful for a while. Kesh Chandra continued to make his house bigger, and he lived happily, away from the temptations of the city.

But soon a month had passed, and the gurumapa was hungry. Kesh Chandra had forgotten to send a meal, so the gurumapa kidnapped one of the village children, and found him very tasty.

The next month, the same thing happened, and then again. Soon, the villagers, including Kesh Chandra, gathered to discuss what could be done.

Kesh Chandra knew he had to take charge, as it was his fault the gurumapa was near the village in the first place, and his fault that he had forgotten to arrange for meals to be prepared for the gurumapa.

He went to see the gurumapa, who had settled in a field nearby. "If the villagers provide you with a huge feast once a year, will you stop eating their children?" asked Kesh Chandra.

The gurumapa had been having a good time eating people, so he wasn't sure. Kesh Chandra, seeing his hesitation, said: "We will give you one buffalo, one bag of rice, black lentils and eighty-four different dishes once a year."

The gurumapa's eyes lit up. Now that was a feast indeed, and it would be far less work to have food brought for him than to have to sneak into the village and hunt down a child to chomp on. He agreed, and so, from that moment on, the villagers made a huge feast every year for the gurumapa, and left it on his field for him to enjoy.

# Royalty

The lives of kings and queens, princes and princesses, are an endless source of fascination. Throw in some magic and some disagreements, and you have the following stories, which are full of fun and adventure, and show that even the rich and powerful can make mistakes and learn from them.

# A Royal Argument

## (PAKISTAN)

*This story is from* The Olive Fairy Book *by Andrew Lang, where it was called "Jackal or Tiger?"*

It was a hot night, and the king and queen of the city lay awake, unable to sleep. The pair had only been married for a few months, and hadn't known each other very well before their marriage. They were both young and headstrong, and prone to arguing, letting their tempers get the best of them, instead of discussing things calmly. That night, with the heat making them restless and the lack of sleep making them annoyed, they were more prone to arguing than usual.

And so, a noise that broke through the silence of the night provided the material for their next argument.

"That," said the king upon hearing the drawn-out howl, "is a tiger."

The queen scoffed. "What are you talking about? It's a jackal."

"No," the king said firmly, raising his voice. He was a young king, and was prone to losing his temper easily, and not used to being wrong. "You are being silly. It is obviously a tiger. How could you think it's a jackal?"

"Because it IS a jackal," said the queen.

"It is a tiger," shouted the king.

"Jackal," replied the queen loudly.

They went back and forth for some moments, getting louder and louder. They could clearly be heard by the guards posted outside the chamber.

Finally, the king got up out of bed. "Fine," he yelled. "Let's ask the guards if it's a tiger or a jackal. If you are right, I will leave immediately and you will be the leader of this kingdom. If I am right, you have to leave immediately, and I will marry someone new."

Now, the guards, as we know from before, had heard every word of the royal couple's argument, including the king's proposed resolution. They knew it was a jackal that had made the howling noise, but they also knew their king was young and headstrong, and would not stick to his word if he was proved wrong. They also knew that if they went against the king and said the howling was from a jackal, they would be punished.

And so, when the king called them inside and asked them what had been making the noise, both guards, without hesitation, said together: "Tiger."

"Ha," said the king to the queen. "I was right. And now you must leave. Guards, escort her out and take her to the forest at the edge of the kingdom."

A palanquin was called, and the queen was

taken far, far away into the forest. There, the guards left her all by herself. It was pitch-dark, and the forest was full of strange noises. The queen found a large tree to shelter beneath, and waited there until morning, crying her eyes out.

As the sun came up, an old man woke up in a cottage nearby. He was used to the sounds of the forest, and this morning, he could hear something different among them, something that sounded like crying. Grabbing his walking stick, the old man left his house and nearby he found the weeping queen.

"Come now, child," said the old man. "Come have a cup of chai with me and my wife, and tell me what is the matter."

The queen followed the old man back to his house, where she drank a warm cup of soothing chai and stilled her tears enough to share her story with the old couple.

"What a fool," the old woman said candidly. "There is nothing for it, you will stay here with us. We will look after you like you are our own daughter."

The queen, whose name was Sadia, was moved, and accepted the couple's offer. She settled into the house and, seven moons later, she welcomed a baby – the king's son. The baby was a boy, and Sadia named him Ameer Ali.

Years passed and the queen and the old couple doted on Ameer. He grew up strong and loved and happy. But as he grew older and explored the forest around him, he found himself itching for adventure. He wanted to go further and further away from home and see what else was out in the world.

For years, his mother and his grandparents – he knew they weren't related by blood, but the old couple gave him love that only grandparents can give – urged him to stay close, and told him the time for adventuring would come. Ameer waited impatiently, and at last he turned eighteen. Knowing they could stop him no longer, his mother and grandparents loaded him up with supplies and sent him on his way, making him promise to never forget them, and to one day come back if he could.

Ameer set off and soon came to the point in the forest he'd never gone beyond. He stepped over the line and was off on his adventures! He saw animals he'd never seen before, and came across new rivers and plants that didn't grow near his home.

After an exhausting day of travelling, Ameer

decided to find something to eat and get some rest. Spotting a pigeon, he grabbed his slingshot and aimed. But instead of hitting the pigeon, he heard a crack and then a shout.

Running to where the noise was coming from, he discovered an old woman hunched over a smashed earthenware pot, water spilled all around her. "Look what you've done," she said to him when he stopped in front of her. "I will have to make a new pot, and I won't have any water for tonight."

The old woman was very cross, but she softened as Ameer began to apologize. "I am so, so sorry," he said sincerely. "It was an accident. To make it up to you, you can have my brass pot which won't break so easily. I will fill it with water for you and carry it back to your house as well."

The old woman was placated, and so, after filling the brass pot with water, she led Ameer back to her house. He set the pot down outside the old woman's cottage, and as he straightened up, he noticed a beautiful young woman peering out from the front door. Ameer hadn't met any young women before, and he didn't know what to say, so he simply turned and began to walk away.

"Wait," called the old woman. "You have shown

me a kindness today. In return, if you ever need help in the forest, all you have to do is call 'Fairy of the forest! Fairy of the forest! Help me now!' And help will come."

Ameer nodded in understanding and continued on his journey. Over the coming weeks and days, he grew closer and closer to the city, until finally he could see the roofs of the houses, and the glittering walls of the palace. A determined young man, Ameer marched up to the palace and waited to be granted an audience with the king.

Once in the throne room, he bowed low. "Your Majesty," he said. "I have come from afar, and I seek a job in your army."

The king's army was strong and full, and there were no jobs going. But Ameer was persistent, and the king agreed, with one caveat. "I will let you join my army, but you must do whatever I command you to do, without hesitation. If you agree, then you can become a soldier."

Ameer agreed immediately, and was sent off to the barracks.

Now, there were two things that Ameer didn't know. Firstly, this king was his father, the man who had thrown his wife out when they argued over whether it was a jackal or a tiger howling outside. Since then, he'd married again, and his wife had brought with her a daughter from her previous marriage. Secondly, Ameer didn't know that the king was scared. For a number of weeks, whenever it was stormy, strange wailing noises had been heard outside the city, but whenever the king sent someone to investigate, they didn't return.

Sure enough, a month after Ameer joined the king's guard, there was a storm and the sound of a woman wailing could be heard in the middle of the night above the wind and the rain. The king sent for his newest soldier, and when Ameer appeared before him, he said: "Do you hear that wailing?"

When Ameer nodded, the king continued: "Take your weapons and find out what is happening. Do not return until you have found out and stopped the wailing. And if you cannot find out, don't return either."

Ameer grabbed his weapons and some supplies, and set off. It was raining and dark, and he was soon soaked through, but he followed the wailing noise as best as he could.

Soon, the noise had grown louder, and in front of him Ameer could see an old woman collapsed by a tree. The noise was clearly coming from her.

Ameer drew closer and caught the woman's attention. "What has happened to make you wail so?" he asked.

The old woman cleared her throat and looked pitifully up at Ameer. "My daughter has been trapped up in this tree for days now. She is badly injured and I have no way to bring her back down; if she is there for much longer, she will die. Please help me bring her down."

Ameer peered up into the tree, and could see something that possibly looked like a person, but also just like a bundle of rags caught on the branches. He was suspicious of the woman's story, and knew he had to exercise caution.

"I will help you," he said to the old woman, who immediately looked relieved. "I will balance myself on my sword for strength, and you can climb up on to my shoulders to reach your daughter."

The old woman agreed, a little too quickly, and the pair got into their positions. But instead of reaching out for her daughter when she got on to Ameer's shoulders, the old woman looped a rope around his neck and began to pull, hoping to knock him out.

Ameer had been right to be suspicious – she was a witch! He quickly flicked his sword up into the air and cut the woman's foot. The rope came loose and the witch disappeared. All that was left behind was a glittering anklet, which Ameer picked up and put in his pocket.

He made his way back to the palace, where everyone was astonished to see him. Kneeling before the king in the throne room, Ameer shared his story and then pulled the anklet out of his pocket. It was a delicate gold chain, with drops of emeralds and rubies attached, the whole thing twinkling like stars in a night sky. The king was so happy that he clapped in delight, and ordered that Ameer be given his own room and a salary raise. And he gave the anklet to his stepdaughter, who was always asking for new jewellery.

The king's stepdaughter was a spoilt young woman who was given everything she wanted and more. In her rooms, she kept two birds, a parrot and a starling. She showed off her new anklet to them that evening, expecting them to coo with praise.

But instead, the pair looked unimpressed. "It's all very well to wear an anklet on your right leg," said the parrot, "but what about the other leg?"

"It looks so bare and empty," added the starling. "You really need a matching anklet."

The princess stormed off to find her stepfather and demand that another anklet be sourced for her. The king was tired of his stepdaughter's ways, but he knew that if she didn't get what she wanted, his wife would be angry with him.

The pair had wed quickly when the king was young and impulsive, but as they had grown older they led largely separate lives. The queen wanted power, which being married to the king gave her, and which she would hopefully cement by marrying her daughter to a powerful man.

The king wanted peace and quiet. As he had grown older and wiser, the king knew that arguments were not often productive, and that winning a disagreement was not the only thing that mattered. Sometimes, letting someone have what they wanted and keeping everyone calm was the best thing.

So he called for Ameer, who had barely had a chance to rest from his last outing. "Go out and find a matching anklet," ordered the king. "And don't bother coming back until you have it."

The next morning, at first light, Ameer left the palace and headed back to the forest. He spent the day searching for a matching anklet. He looked under plants and fallen branches; he climbed trees to look among their leaves; he lifted rocks by the water. But there was no sign of a matching anklet.

Ameer was almost ready to give up when he remembered the old woman and her instructions for if he ever needed help. He made his way to her house and once outside, stood and called: "Fairy of the forest! Fairy of the forest! Help me now!"

He'd barely finished speaking before the door opened and out stepped the beautiful woman Ameer had seen the last time he'd been at the house. Unlike their last encounter, this time Ameer was able to say hello and explain his predicament.

The young woman nodded. "I can help you," she said, bustling about and moving a few things into place. "Here's what you're going to do. I am going to lie between these two wands. You will cut off my foot, and squeeze the blood out into this cauldron. What will fall will be jewels. After you have done this, change the position of the wands and hold my foot to the wound, and it will heal."

Ameer was horrified. "I can't do that," he said

quietly. "I don't want to hurt you."

"It won't hurt me," said the woman. "And it's the only way to get the jewels you need."

And so, reluctantly, Ameer agreed. The woman lay between the two wands and, taking a deep breath, Ameer cut off her foot, quickly taking it to the cauldron and squeezing. Before his very eyes, instead of blood, out fell some jewels. Ameer swapped the wands, held the woman's foot to her wound, and watched as the cut stitched itself back together.

The young woman stood up. "See?" she said. "All done, and I am completely fine. Now, take the jewels and have them set into an anklet for the princess."

Ameer grabbed the jewels and left, with one last glance behind him to wave at the woman. He hurried back to the city, had the jewels set into an anklet, and then made his way to the throne room to present them to the king.

That evening, after the princess had returned to her room with the second anklet, she showed off to her birds.

"Hmm, yes," said the parrot. "I suppose that the two anklets do look good, but…"

"But what?" shouted the princess.

"Well," said the starling. "Your ankles look great, but now your wrists and throat look so empty. It's a pity you don't have a matching necklace and bracelets."

The princess stomped off to see her mother, who heard her daughter's complaints and immediately demanded of her husband that a matching necklace and bracelet be found.

And so, once again, the king called for Ameer. And, once again, Ameer headed into the forest.

This time, he didn't waste hours searching, but instead headed to the house of the young woman. Once outside, he called: "Fairy of the forest! Fairy of the forest! Help me now!"

The door opened and the young woman stepped outside. Ameer explained that he needed more jewels. Expecting to do exactly the same as last time, Ameer was shocked when the woman said that this time he would need to cut off her hands and head. It took a long time for the woman to persuade Ameer that she'd be OK, but finally he agreed to go ahead.

Everything proceeded exactly as before, and the wounds on the woman's wrists and neck healed so quickly it was like nothing had happened. Bidding the woman goodbye, Ameer headed to the city, had the jewels set into bracelets and a necklace, and handed them to the king. Then he went to have a well-deserved nap.

The princess received her jewellery from the king and headed back to her room with it, where she modelled it for her birds. They oohed and aahed over it for a while.

"But…" said the starling shortly. The princess stopped her twirling immediately.

"All that pretty jewellery," said the parrot, "and nowhere for you to wear it. Surely the only suitable place would be your own wedding. And the only person worthy of marrying you is the man who found you those bracelets and necklace and anklets."

And so, the princess stormed off to see the king, and demanded that Ameer Ali become her husband. This, thought the king, was something he could quite easily do. But when Ameer came before him and heard the king's request, he refused.

"What?" said the king, completely stunned.

"I am already falling in love," said Ameer. "And I cannot marry any other woman. Your Majesty, I apologize, but I cannot go against my heart."

The queen scoffed. "You are being asked to marry the princess of the realm," she said in her haughty voice. "How dare you turn down this chance? My daughter is beautiful, and you are but a soldier; you should know how lucky you are to have her."

Ameer turned to the queen and bowed, hoping to placate her. "My queen, if it were anything else, I would do my best to grant your request, but this is one thing I cannot do."

The queen grew angrier; she was desperate for her daughter to gain more power and she knew a marriage was, unfortunately, the only way to gain the throne. "This is insubordination. We will not stand for it, will we, husband?"

The king, not knowing what else to do and with his wife and her daughter very clearly fuming beside him, ordered Ameer be taken to the jail. There, he would remain for the rest of his life.

Now, Ameer's story had spread far and wide. People were impressed by his bravery in beating the witch, and by his loyalty to the woman he loved. People in the city talked about him, and merchants visiting took his story out to other parts of the kingdom, until soon, an old couple and their adopted daughter heard the tale.

The king regularly heard petitions from his subjects, and one day, a few weeks after Ameer was put in jail, an old man was brought before him, accompanied by his wife and another, younger, woman, who seemed to be their daughter.

"Your Majesty," said the old man. "I have come to tell you that the tiger only hunts in the forest, while the jackal hunts wherever there is something to be gained. Jackals have turned up to claim the throne, but you shouldn't mistake a jackal for a tiger for the second time."

The crowd of courtiers watching were puzzled. What on earth was this man going on about? But the king understood the reference immediately; he had never forgotten the argument he'd had with his first wife, and now he was wiser, he regretted how cruelly he'd treated her.

"The jackal," continued the old man, "has returned."

The king cleared the throne room immediately, and asked the old man to explain. And so, the man told of how he had come across a weeping woman, and how he and his wife had taken that woman in and helped her bring up her baby, who had grown into a fine and honourable young man.

And then, even before the younger woman had lowered her hood, the king understood. Before him stood his former wife, looking older than when he had last seen her, but no less regal.

"Ameer Ali is our son," the former queen said. "He has been nothing but loyal to you, and you have jailed him for not giving in to the demands of your petty wife and stepdaughter, who have had their eyes on your throne for quite a while."

The king was embarrassed, for he knew he'd done poorly by his family. He had first let his ego get in the way, resulting in the banishment of his first wife, and then he had been too cowardly to stand up to a power-hungry wife and stepdaughter.

Full of remorse, the king ordered the immediate release of Ameer. He begged forgiveness from his son who, having been brought up to be a kind young man, granted that forgiveness immediately.

And, after many years in an unhappy marriage, he decided to have a proper conversation with his wife.

"We have both been miserable for many years," the king said. He could see his wife getting angry, so he quickly carried on. "But, my dear, I believe we should be more honest with each other; it is time for us to divorce. You should know that your daughter will not take over this throne, but I will not be so cruel as to throw a second wife out of the kingdom. I will provide a home for you and your daughter, but you will no longer interfere with the palace workings."

The queen was stunned at this decisive and confident and honest king, so stunned that she had no comeback. She simply went to get her daughter and start packing so they could move.

Over the coming weeks, the king and Ameer got to know one another, and Ameer also regularly called upon the fairy of the forest. They soon fell properly in love, and decided to get married. The king hosted a large celebration and, as his wedding present, he crowned his son the new king, knowing he would be a fair and kind ruler.

# Rama and Sita

*This story is based on The Ramayana, a Hindu epic which tells the story of Rama, an incarnation of the god Vishnu. It also features Sita, his wife, who is the mother goddess and a form of Lakshmi, who is married to Vishnu. The original epic is huge: it consists of twenty-four thousand verses!*

*There are many variations of this story, which has also been depicted in numerous works of art – especially paintings – and inspired television series.*

*All of the stories end in a similar way, with a path home being lit by small lanterns called diya. This part of the story has particular significance to the Hindu festival of Diwali, the festival of lights, which takes place in late autumn or early winter in the Western calendar.*

Rama, the oldest and favourite son of the king of the ancient city of Ayodhya, was a brave and fearsome warrior, loved by his people. There was great rejoicing when he married Sita, a kind woman known for her dedication and courage.

Rama's stepmother, however, did not like the pair, because she wanted her own son to be the future king. Knowing Rama and Sita were popular with the people, she decided to persuade the king to banish the pair.

"Rama has spent all his time as a warrior," she whispered to the king constantly. "He has no experience of living independently, and he could never be a good king if he can't think for himself."

Her cunning worked, and the king had soon decided to banish Rama and Sita for fourteen years. And so Rama, a loyal son, agreed, and he and Sita found a distant forest to live in. Living with them was Laksmana, Rama's younger brother, who willingly exiled himself because of his loyalty to and love for his sibling.

For a long time, the trio lived a simple and happy life in a humble cottage, surrounded by nature: glorious trees, sparkling waters, and animals, birds and insects whose beauty shone through every day.

Seasons passed and came around again, and Rama, Sita and Laksmana were content with their humble lives. They enjoyed being surrounded by nature and getting to know the animals and plants they shared their home with, often indulging in long walks to try and find new parts of the forest that they hadn't seen yet.

But, unknown to them, their life soon attracted the attention of Ravana, the demon king. He had spotted Sita walking in the forest one day and, drawn in by her kindness towards the animals, decided he wanted to marry her. Ravana had ten heads and twenty arms, and could change his body into whatever form he wanted, and decided to use this to his advantage to trick Sita.

The next time he saw Sita out on a walk, Ravana transformed into a graceful yet injured deer. After he was sure Sita had spotted him, he disappeared into the woods, making sure Sita could see the deer's limp and the wound on its back. He knew that Sita's caring nature meant she would not be able to resist helping, and that she would not forget the injured deer once it disappeared from her sight.

Sita searched for the deer, hoping to help it return to full health, but to no avail. She eventually returned home and Rama could immediately see she was upset.

He took her into his arms. "What has saddened you so, my love?" he asked, letting go of her and moving to sit them both down.

"I saw an injured deer in the forest," Sita said. "It had a wound on its back that looked so painful – it was still bleeding. And it was limping as well, as though it had badly hurt its foot or leg. I searched all afternoon for it, but I haven't been able to find it. I'm worried sick that its injuries will get worse and it will die."

Rama knew that he could make Sita happy and help the deer. He leaped up. "This is a problem that can be solved," he said, moving to gather some supplies. "I'll hunt for the deer and bring it back here, so we can nurse it back to health together."

Rama decided to take Laksmana with him, and the two prepared for their journey. But before he left, Rama drew a circle of magic around Sita. "This is a circle of protection," he told Sita. "If you remain inside it, no harm will come to you. But if you step outside of the circle and encounter danger, I will not be able to help you."

Sita promised to remain inside the circle, and

Rama and Laksmana left. After a little time had passed, Sita saw an old man wander down the path to her home. She watched him from her protective circle, seeing his stooped shoulders, his slow gait and his shaky hands on the walking stick he clutched.

"Old man," Sita called, "you look tired and hungry; you should rest and eat some food. There is a stream nearby where you can find water."

The old man looked up at Sita. "I am too frail to make it to the stream," he said. "Will you fetch me a glass of water?"

Seeing his wrinkled face and watery eyes, Sita thought there was no danger he could pose to her. And so kind-hearted Sita decided she would get the old man his water, knowing that Rama could not blame her for stepping out of the circle to help someone so in need.

As soon as Sita's second foot left the circle, Ravana transformed back into his ten-headed, twenty-armed self and grabbed Sita. An initial jolt of fear turned into dismay; Sita knew she had been tricked and that she was in danger. Quickly, Ravana summoned his pushpak, a chariot that he could control with his thoughts. Tossing Sita on to it, he climbed up and whisked her away.

When Rama and Laksmana returned, having seen no sign at all of the deer, they discovered Sita was missing. Rama realized that there was no one else who had the power to cause such a disappearance but Ravana and knew he and Sita had been tricked. An anger flowed through him towards the demon king. Fuelled by his rage, and by his love for Sita and desire to get her back safely, he and Laksmana set about combing through the forest to find her.

They looked at the ground for footprints, at the trees and plants for broken branches, but could find no sign of where Ravana had taken Sita. Soon, they came upon Hanuman, the wise and resourceful king of the monkeys. He gave them shelter and food, and they explained what had happened to Sita.

Hanuman trusted Rama; he knew Sita to be a generous and brave person, and so he agreed to help straight away. He called on the monkeys to begin the search, knowing that if they could not find out what happened, no one could. The monkeys combed the forest from the treetops and the ground and soon found a faint trail. They followed it and discovered that Ravana was hiding Sita on his island home of Lanka.

There, in a prison cell unseen by the monkeys, Sita calmly sat. She had refused to speak to Ravana since he had imprisoned her, holding on to her courage when the demon king tried to threaten her. She knew if she waited and believed, rescue would come.

Meanwhile, the monkeys had returned to tell Hanuman, Rama and Laksmana what they had discovered.

"But," said Rama, "how do we get on to the island? We have no vessels to carry us across the water, and no way to fly."

Hanuman thought for a moment, and then his eyes lit up. "We will build a bridge."

And so the monkeys, Rama and Laksmana set about gathering materials from the forest. They tied together pieces of wood, made rope from plants and used magic to weave together the materials and infuse it with strength, and bit by bit, their bridge came together. As the last parts of the bridge slotted into place, Ravana discovered their plan, thanks to his legion of soldiers. Making sure Sita was securely locked up, he gathered his demon army and went out to meet Hanuman and Rama's army of monkeys.

And so a fierce battle began. They fought with swords, and they fought with their hands, and they fought with their magic, both sides never giving up. The battle raged for ten long days and nights, and while both armies began to get tired and sustain wounds, it was the monkey army that suffered more. It looked as though the demon king Ravana would triumph.

But Rama was determined to win and find Sita, and he issued a challenge to Ravana to battle him one on one.

"If you think you can beat me, just try!" he shouted at Ravana over the noise of the fighting.

Not one to back down from a challenge, Ravana accepted, and the pair met on the battlefield with their astras, weapons containing magical energy. They parried and dodged, swiping at each other and missing, but never giving up. Finally Rama cut off one of Ravana's heads, thinking he had become victorious. But as he watched, another head grew back in its place. Rama cut a second head off, and in the time it took to fall to the floor, Ravana grew one back in its place.

The fight was ferocious, with Rama injuring Ravana again and again, but Ravana survived each time. Finally, Rama decided to use a magic arrow, which he shot at Ravana. The demon king finally stumbled, for Rama had caught him in the one place where he could be killed. As Rama and the armies watched, Ravana faded before their eyes, and died.

Seeing their king was dead, the demon army withdrew, and the monkey army swarmed the island of Lanka, looking for Sita's cell. When they found it, they freed her and she ran to Rama, embracing him tightly. They both had tears streaming down their faces with joy at their reunion.

"I'm so happy you're OK," Rama whispered to Sita. "But I knew your bravery would see you through."

"Not just my bravery," said Sita through her tears. "I believed you would stop at nothing to help me, and that thought sustained me."

There was much rejoicing as the pair were reunited. Everyone cheered and clapped and sang as they made their way over the bridge, leaving Lanka and the battle behind them.

Hanuman, Rama, Sita and Laksmana walked back through the forest, and soon came to Hanuman's and the monkeys' home. There, they bid Hanuman farewell, promising to see each other again. Their friendship had seen many hardships, and was stronger for the battle they had fought together.

Rama, Sita and Laksmana carried on, deciding to make their way back to the palace now that their fourteen years of exile were over. As they walked, darkness began to fall. To aid them in their journey, the animals and people along the way lit diya, small lanterns, for them. As more people caught sight of the lanterns, more and more were lit, until a path was illuminated through the darkness all the way to the palace.

Rama, Sita and Laksmana eventually made it home. The king was ecstatic to see his sons and his daughter-in-law, and hugged all three tightly. "Welcome home, my sons. You are a sight for sore eyes," the king said to Rama and Laksmana. "And daughter-in-law," the king continued, "this is your home as much as it is my boys'. I welcome you back."

When the king had discovered his wife's cunning plan, he had thwarted it and banished his wife and her son. As many years had passed, he knew Rama, Sita and Laksmana would soon return, and he settled patiently to wait for them. He was ready to see Rama take the throne after him, especially after his son had been so loyal to him.

And so, the kingdom greeted the trio like heroes, welcoming them home through the darkness with light.

# The Cat Who Became Queen

## (KASHMIR)

*This tale is part of a tradition – found across the world – of stories about animals that become royals. It was originally told in Folk-Tales of Kashmir by J. Hinton Knowles, a British missionary in Kashmir in the nineteenth century.*

Once upon a time, there was a king who had almost everything he wanted. He had a large and peaceful kingdom. He had happy subjects. He had wealth beyond compare.

But there was one thing he didn't have, and it was one thing he wanted above all else: an heir. The king had many wives (this was a long time ago, when kings were allowed many wives) and none had borne him a child.

The king really, really wanted a son, someone he could hand his kingdom over to, and one day, he decided he'd had enough.

"That's it," he shouted, storming into the massive wing of the palace where all his wives lived. Each had their own rooms, but they were all gathered together in the courtyard, sewing and talking and eating. When they heard the king's shout, they all fell silent and stopped what they were doing.

"I have had enough," the king bellowed, his voice echoing off the stone walls and scaring the birds out of the trees. "If I do not have a son within a year, I will banish you all."

And with that, he stormed off. For a moment, silence reigned, and then all the king's wives began talking at once.

"What shall we do?"

"We can't be banished!"

"This is a disaster!"

Once they had calmed down, the wives decided they would pray. And so, for the weeks and months to come, they prayed and prayed, but nothing happened.

The year was almost up – there were just a few days to go – when good news reached the king. One of his wives had given birth to a baby girl!

Now, the king very much wanted a son, but he supposed a girl would do. He would make sure she wanted for nothing, and then he would find someone equal to her to marry her, and he would give his kingdom to his future son-in-law.

The king rejoiced at his good fortune, and then, unsurprisingly, he asked for his baby daughter to be brought to him so he could meet her properly.

A message came back from the wives: "The Brahmans say the baby cannot be seen by anyone but us until she is married."

Not wanting to put his daughter or his kingdom's future in jeopardy, the king agreed.

But it wasn't the Brahmans who had decided the king couldn't see his daughter. It was his wives.

And the reason they didn't want the king to see his daughter was because there was no baby.

Well, that wasn't technically true. There was a baby, she just didn't belong to one of the wives. And she wasn't a human but a kitten!

One of the palace cats had given birth to a litter of kittens, and the wives had adopted the smallest one. And that kitten was the "daughter" they had told the king about.

As the years passed, the king received messages about his daughter's health and well-being. He was told she grew strong and brave and clever. She loved to read and write, she was accomplished with a sword and a bow, and she was growing up tall and beautiful.

In reality, all that was happening was that the kitten had grown into a cat – a beautiful cat, but still a cat nonetheless. Luckily, no one else had discovered the secret the wives had been keeping.

It was only a matter of time until their luck ran out, and that day came on the date the king thought was his daughter's eighteenth birthday. On that day, he sent a message to the wives telling them he had arranged for his daughter to marry the prince of a nearby kingdom.

The wives, once again, panicked.

"He'll banish us when he finds out we lied!"

"He'll do more than banish us, he'll threaten to execute us!"

"What shall we do?"

The wives pondered their dilemma through the day and the night, discussing many different approaches. In the end, they decided the only thing to do was to confide in the prince, and make him promise not to tell anyone anything about what they had revealed to him.

The prince was a kind young man, and when he arrived at the palace for the wedding, he was granted an audience with the wives. They told him about their ruse and showed him the cat they had adopted. They told the prince that they were sure the king would punish them harshly, and that if he was as kind-hearted as his reputation said he was, he would keep their secret.

The prince had no wish to see anyone harmed, and agreed to keep their secret. When he saw the king that evening, he said that he wanted a private wedding, with only the royal women of the household present, and that immediately afterwards he and the king's "daughter" would leave in a covered carriage.

The king, who knew the prince was an excellent catch, didn't want to protest anything that would make him back out of the marriage, so agreed to every demand.

The wedding took place quickly, and soon the prince was on his way home, with the cat beside him in the carriage. When he arrived back at his kingdom, he snuck the cat into his wing of the palace and told his mum and dad – the king and queen – that his wife was very shy, and didn't want to ever see anyone else.

The king and queen were puzzled, but they loved their son and didn't want to make their daughter-in-law uncomfortable, so they agreed. But the prince's mum dearly wanted the new princess to feel welcome and so, one day when the prince was out meeting the people of the kingdom, she knocked on the princess's bedroom door.

"My dear," the queen called through it, "I know you are very shy, but everyone has gone out. It is just you and me here. Will you come out?"

After spending years living with the wives, the cat could understand everything humans said, and on hearing the queen's words, she wept with unhappiness and loneliness. Her cries went straight to the queen's heart, who resolved to speak to her son to see what could be done.

The cat's cries were also heard by the benevolent deity Parvati, who was moved by the cat's longing to be human. She went to her husband, the powerful god Shiva, and said: "Is there nothing we can do to help this poor cat?"

Shiva thought for a moment. "Tell the cat to rub oil all over her fur," he said, "and she will become human."

Parvati took the message back to the cat, who followed the instructions, covering all but a tiny patch of fur on her shoulder with oil. Within moments, she'd turned into a young woman.

When the prince came back that night, he was astonished to find this woman in his quarters. "It's me," said the princess hurriedly. "I have turned from a cat into a human, and look, to prove it to you, here's a patch of my old fur which remains on my shoulder."

And she showed him the fur. The prince was stunned, but sat with the woman and they talked all night – telling each other about their lives, and sharing their secrets. That night, the prince fell in love with the woman, and the woman fell in love with the prince.

Their joy was such that they couldn't contain it, and they agreed that the woman – the princess – should meet the king and queen, who were ecstatic that their daughter-in-law had decided to come out to see them, her shyness mostly gone.

And after a number of weeks there, the couple journeyed to the princess's kingdom, where the king finally met his daughter (no one told him she used to be a cat, though) and the wives were overjoyed that their wild plan had somehow worked in their favour.

And when the time came, the princess's father and the prince's father gave their kingdoms to the prince. And the couple ruled happily for years. Together.

# The Three Princes

## (PAKISTAN)

This is a story from The Arabian Nights, *the famous collection of stories narrated by Sheherazade, who told a story each night to her husband, the king, leaving it on a cliffhanger so he would let her live another night because he wanted to hear the next instalment so badly.*

*It's actually part of a bigger story called "Prince Ahmad and the Fairy Paribanou" (which is the next story in this book), but the first part is about a trio of brothers, and works well on its own.*

Once upon a time, there was a sultan who had three sons: Prince Husain, Prince Ali and Prince Ahmad. The brothers were not far apart in age, and they were companions and friends as well as brothers.

Living with them was Princess Nur-al-Nihar, the daughter of their father's late friend. When his friend died, the sultan had taken Princess Nur-al-Nihar in, and brought her up alongside his sons.

Over the years, all three of the brothers fell in love with Princess Nur-al-Nihar. The princess also loved all the princes equally, and when they and the princess came of age, she was torn between who would be the best match for her.

Deciding to talk to the sultan, she revealed her dilemma to him. All of the princes were accomplished and clever and kind and brave, and Princess Nur-al-Nihar could not choose between them. So, with the sultan, she decided to set them a challenge.

"The three of you will journey out into the world," the sultan told them. "You will spend a year, each of you in a different place, and try and find the rarest item you can. When you all return, you will present these items to me and the princess, and whoever brings us the most impressive item will marry Nur-al-Nihar."

"As well as completing the challenge, the year apart will give all of us time to grow," said Princess Nur-al-Nihar. "We will have our own adventures, independent of each other, and it will give us the chance to assess our feelings."

The three princes agreed and readied to leave, making sure they had enough money and the best horses. After saying goodbye, they set off.

For a while, the trio travelled together, until one evening they came to a crossroads where the path split into three. There was an inn at this crossroads.

"Let us stay here for the night," said Prince Husain. "In the morning we will split up and go our separate ways."

The others agreed, and they all indulged in a hearty meal. Despite the fact they were in competition with one another, the brothers got on well and there was plenty of laughter that evening.

After a good night's sleep, the trio gathered at the crossroads.

"Let us agree," said Prince Ali, "to meet back here in a year. We will show each other our rare items, and then make our way back home together."

Prince Ahmad nodded. "Whoever arrives first must wait for the second," he said. "And those two must then wait for the third of us."

The brothers all shook hands and embraced, and then made off on their separate paths.

Prince Husain took the route to Bishangarh. He travelled part of the way on his own, before joining a caravan heading towards the town. His journey wasn't terribly long, and it only took him a few weeks to arrive.

Once there, he was greeted with the sight of a huge and bustling bazaar. There were merchants selling rich cloths and unusual jewels, exquisite pottery and handmade crafts.

Through the noise, he heard a carpet seller: "Come buy my carpet! Thirty thousand gold pieces! Carpet for thirty thousand gold pieces."

Prince Husain was stunned. What kind of carpet cost thirty thousand gold pieces? Yes, this was a pretty carpet. It was a deep midnight-blue colour that looked rich and warm, and all around the edge were spiral patterns in gold thread, and gold tassels adorned each of the four corners. In the centre was a large gold star surrounded by tiny gold stars. It almost looked like a night sky. Yes, it was a pretty carpet, but even a pretty carpet would be a fraction of the price the merchant was advertising.

Curious, he made his way to the seller. "O Merchant," he said as he approached. "Why are you selling a carpet for thirty thousand gold pieces? Surely you are being silly."

The merchant invited the prince to sit down. "This is no ordinary carpet," he said. "This carpet will take you anywhere you want to go."

A flying carpet? Prince Husain was sceptical, and his face showed it. "I can see you don't believe me," said the merchant. "I am happy for you to try it out. All we have to do is sit on the carpet, and you have to think about where you would like to go. And then the carpet will take us there."

Prince Husain was still disbelieving, but there was no harm in trying it. "If this carpet does as you say, merchant," he said, "then I will buy it from you for forty thousand gold pieces, for it will be worth that much."

Prince Husain and the merchant settled themselves on the carpet, and then Prince Husain pictured in his mind the desert just outside the vast city, which was a day's ride away. Barely a moment passed before he felt a jolt, and the carpet was moving through the air faster than any horse could move or any bird could fly. Within seconds, Prince Husain and the merchant were in the desert, exactly as Prince Husain had pictured.

The prince was astonished and impressed. *This carpet is surely unique*, he said to himself. To the merchant, he said: "You have proven yourself true. Let us go back to the bazaar, and I will give you the promised forty thousand gold pieces."

Prince Husain thought of the merchant's stall in the bazaar, and before the thought was even complete, the carpet was on the move. Seconds later, they were back in the bazaar, where the prince handed over forty thousand gold pieces. The merchant rolled the carpet up for him, and Prince Husain took it to his lodgings.

He had found his item very quickly, and so decided to spend some time exploring Bishangarh, seeing the sights, trying lots of different food and meeting new people. After a few months, satisfied he had made the most of his time in Bishangarh, he got his carpet, loaded all his belongings and his horse on to it, stepped on it and thought of the inn where he and his brothers agreed to meet. In a flash, the carpet had transported him there. He was the first to return, so he took up a room in the inn, where he would remain until his brothers arrived.

Meanwhile, Prince Ali had taken the second path at the crossroads, and travelled a lot further than his older brother. Joining a caravan, he had made his way to Shiraz in Iran. Arriving there, he went to the bustling bazaar, where he heard of a man selling a tube for thirty thousand gold pieces.

What kind of tube is worth thirty thousand gold pieces? Prince Ali was curious, and so went to find the merchant.

"O Merchant," said Prince Ali. "I hear tell that you are selling a tube for thirty thousand gold pieces. What does this tube do to make it so special?"

The merchant showed Prince Ali the tube, which looked like any other spyglass the royal had seen. "This is no ordinary spyglass," said the merchant. "If you hold it to your eye and think of what you want to see, this tube will show it to you, even if it is thousands of leagues away."

Prince Ali had said nothing for a few moments.

"I can see that you don't believe me," said the merchant. "I am happy for you to try the tube to see it at work."

Prince Ali took the tube from the merchant. "If it works, Merchant," said Prince Ali, "then I will give you forty thousand gold pieces, for surely it is worth that."

The prince held the tube up to his right eye, shut his left eye and thought of his home — first he thought of his father in his throne room. Before his very eye, the tube showed him his father sitting on his throne, consulting with his advisors. Prince Ali pulled the tube away from his face quickly, but yes, he was still in the bazaar.

He brought the tube back to his right eye, and this time thought of Princess Nur-al-Nihar in her favourite place, the palace gardens. And there she was! He could see her with her friends and attendants, planting roses.

The prince turned to the merchant. "You have spoken true," he said. "This spyglass is extraordinary and I will give you forty thousand gold pieces for it."

The pair made the exchange, and the prince took the spyglass back to his lodgings, where he began making his preparations for the long journey home. He set off and, at the crossroads, he was greeted by Prince Husain. Together, they settled in at the inn to await the arrival of their youngest brother.

Prince Ahmad had taken the third and final path, which led him to the legendary city of Samarkand, far, far away from his home. After resting from his long journey, the prince went off in search of an unusual item to take back home to his father.

He searched high and low through the city's many large bazaars, and eventually heard a rumour about a merchant selling an apple for thirty thousand gold pieces. An apple for thirty thousand gold pieces? It was so ridiculous that Prince Ahmad knew he had to find out more.

After asking many people, Prince Ahmad eventually found the merchant. "O Merchant," he said. "I have heard tell of an apple you are selling for thirty thousand gold pieces. Tell me, what kind of apple is worth that much?"

"This is no ordinary apple," said the merchant, holding out something that did, actually, look like an ordinary apple, if a little redder and shinier and plumper. "This apple was created by a sage who lived in this city many years ago. When he got very old and felt he had lived a full life and was ready to die, he decided to sell the apple and give the money to his family. If anyone falls ill, even if they are moments from death, one scent of this apple and they will be cured."

The prince was sceptical, but while the merchant had told his story, a crowd had gathered. "My neighbour is gravely ill," said a woman in the crowd. "Will this apple cure her?"

"It will," said the merchant. "Let us go and try it, and then, prince, you will see that it works."

"If it works," said the prince, "I will give you forty thousand gold pieces for the apple, for it will surely be worth that much."

So the merchant, the prince and the crowd of people followed the woman to her neighbour's house. Inside, the prince and the merchant found a young woman whose breathing was rattling in her chest.

The merchant approached, and held the apple under the woman's nose. In the space of one breath, colour came back to the woman's cheeks, and she blinked her eyes open and sat straight up. Her husband and children, who had been crying at her bedside, were astounded and hugged her tightly.

Prince Ahmad turned to the merchant. "You have proven the worth of your apple," he said. "Let us go back to your stall and I will give you the forty thousand gold pieces I promised."

The pair returned to the merchant's shop and Prince Ahmad handed over the money. It had taken him a long time to find the apple, so he hastily packed his belongings and set off on the return journey to the crossroads.

On arrival, his two older brothers were waiting for him, and they all embraced. After sharing a meal together, they retired to discuss their adventures, before moving on to showing each other their goods.

"I bought a carpet," said Prince Husain. "If one sits on it and thinks of where they would like to go, the carpet transports you there in an instant."

His brothers were impressed, and Prince Husain promised them they could try it out soon.

Prince Ali showed them the spyglass. "This tube will show you anything you want to look at, even if it is thousands of miles away," he said. "All you have to do is think of the person or place you would like to see."

He handed it to Prince Husain to try, and the oldest of the brothers thought of the palace. But when he looked through the spyglass, what he saw scared him.

"Everyone looks worried," he told his brothers. "Something has clearly happened."

Prince Ali took the spyglass and thought of his father, but the spyglass showed the sultan looking panicked, but otherwise healthy.

"Perhaps something is wrong with Princess Nur-al-Nihar," said Prince Husain, taking the spyglass back. And sure enough, when he thought of the princess and looked through it, it was to see her lying on her bed, surrounded by attendants. The princess looked gravely ill, and her servants and friends were crying.

He told his brothers what he had seen. "What can we do? We have no cure," said Prince Ali.

Prince Ahmad held out his apple. "This apple will cure anyone, no matter how ill they are, if you hold it under their nose and let them catch its scent," he said.

"Well, there's nothing for it," said Prince Husain. "Let us all get on my carpet, and it will take us to the princess instantly, and we can administer this cure."

The men sat on the carpet and within seconds were in the princess's quarters, shocking everyone in the room with their sudden arrival. But there was no time for surprise or explanation at this point; Prince Ahmad leaped off the carpet and made his way to where the princess lay.

He held the apple underneath her nose, and everyone watched as the princess regained her colour and opened her eyes almost immediately. She sat up, and it was as though no illness had befallen her; she was the picture of health.

The sultan was overjoyed at the princess's recovery. He drew her into his arms, unable to believe that she looked so hale and hearty so suddenly.

"How do you feel?" he asked her, looking carefully at her face for any signs of pain.

The princess rolled her neck, and stretched her arms above her head before getting out of bed and walking around the room while everyone watched. "I feel fine," she said, with a trace of amazement in her voice. "I feel no pain in my head or my muscles. In fact, I feel healthier than I've ever felt!"

She embraced the sultan again, and then hugged the three princes and her attendants, overjoyed at the return of her health.

After celebrating for a while, the sultan and his sons left the princess, insisting that even though she felt well she should rest after her illness. It also gave the sultan the chance to welcome his sons home properly; he was ecstatic to see them after a year apart.

But as they told him about their travels, and showed him their items, he became increasingly worried. All three – the carpet, the spyglass and the apple – were unique, and without all three of them, the princess would not have been saved.

Knowing it was impossible for he and Princess Nur-al-Nihar to pick between his sons, the sultan went to talk to the princess. Together, they decided on a final contest to choose who would marry Princess Nur-al-Nihar: each of the princes would shoot an arrow. Whoever shot furthest would win the princess's hand.

The princes, the sultan and their attendants headed to the shooting range. Prince Husain, as the eldest, went first, and shot his arrow a good distance.

Prince Ali was next, and his arrow went further than his older brother's.

Finally, Prince Ahmad stepped up. When he shot his arrow, it disappeared into the distance. The sultan's attendants searched for it fruitlessly, but after many hours it still could not be found. As it was impossible to measure the distance of Prince Ahmad's arrow, the sultan declared Prince Ali as the winner.

Princess Nur-al-Nihar was glad, for Prince Ali was a fine man and she loved him very much. The two often lost themselves in long conversations with each other, and they had many hobbies in common, from horse riding to gardening. But they were also quite different, and she knew she would never be bored in his presence. Their wedding was a joyous celebration, for nearly everyone.

Prince Husain, wounded at his loss, went to live as a fakir, renouncing all his worldly goods and embracing spirituality. And Prince Ahmad? Well, his story is for another time.

# Prince Ahmad and the Fairy Peribanou

## (PAKISTAN)

*This story continues the tale of Prince Ahmad from* The Arabian Nights.

Prince Ahmad was hunting. He had celebrated the marriage of his older brother, Prince Ali, to the Princess Nur-al-Nihar and, although he had loved the princess and wanted to marry her, he was happy seeing his brother's happiness.

But now the celebrations were over, and Prince Ahmad was hunting. Not for animals, but for an arrow. Specifically, the arrow that he'd shot in the contest to win Princess Nur-al-Nihar's hand in marriage, and that had disappeared completely from sight.

The prince had set off on his journey a short time ago, but he'd already walked much further than any arrow could go. But with no sign of it – not on the ground, or caught up in a bush, or wedged in the trunk of a tree – he continued on.

When he had gone about three parasangs (a very long way), he caught a flash of something on a rock ahead. As he approached, he saw that it was his arrow! But how had it flown so far? And how had it landed perfectly on this rock?

Prince Ahmad picked up the arrow and looked around him until he caught sight of a path disappearing between some large rocks. He followed it, and found a gap in the ground that led to an underground passage. At the end of the passage, he could see an iron door. It was rather plain: a dull bronze in colour, but it was large and looked strong and sturdy.

He approached cautiously and gently tapped on the door. The thudding sound it made clued him in to the fact that it was thick. Prince Ahmad pushed at the door, expecting nothing to happen, but it gave way under his hand. He stepped through it, expecting to find himself in a dark cavern. But instead, the room was brightly lit and huge, and just up ahead he could see an extraordinary, glittering palace.

Prince Ahmad walked forward, and when he was a short way from the palace, he was stopped by the sight of a woman walking out to greet him. She was a beautiful fairy, as tall as he was. She had dark brown skin that glowed, and long, thick hair that was tied in a plait running down to the small of her back. Some loose curls framed her full face, and her dark brown eyes were piercing yet welcoming in their gaze.

"Prince Ahmad, you have made it at last," she said in a soothing voice. "I have waited for a long time for you."

Prince Ahmad bowed to the fairy, curious as to how she knew his name. The fairy, seeing the puzzlement on his face, beckoned him forward and into the palace, where the pair settled on a fluffy rug.

"I am the fairy Peribanou," the fairy said. "I am the daughter of a jinn chief, and I have been aware of your existence for a long time. It is I who commanded your arrow be carried this great distance, in the hope you would find me. Only those who I allow can see the iron door; to all others it is just a wall of rock. It is my wish to marry you."

Prince Ahmad was stunned, and could feel himself falling for Peribanou. "But," he said, concerned about one thing, "will your family accept your marriage to me? Do they not want you to marry someone from another jinn family?"

Peribanou smiled. "In our world, it is up to people to choose for themselves who they marry," she explained. "I have chosen you, and my family will be happy with this choice, because it makes me happy. I realize this is sudden for you, so take your time."

In the coming days, Prince Ahmad got to know the fair Peribanou. He learned she was very quick-witted and funny, and that he could talk to her about any subject. Peribanou was kind to all around her, and worked hard to make sure her people were happy.

And so, after some time had passed, Peribanou and Prince Ahmad decided to get married. They had a huge wedding celebration, filled with laughter and joy and lots of food. Prince Ahmad got to know everyone in Peribanou's court, and settled into life in the palace very quickly.

A few months passed, and while Prince Ahmad was more deeply in love with Peribanou than ever, he could not help but let a sadness pass over him. He missed his father and wondered how he was faring.

What he wasn't to know is that his father, the sultan, had also been feeling a similar sadness. His middle son, Prince Ali, was happily married to Princess Nur-al-Nihar. The pair did not like the bustle of the city or the politics of court, and lived peacefully in the countryside. The sultan's oldest son, Prince Husain, had renounced his status and his worldly goods and embraced his spirituality to become a fakir, and of his younger, Prince Ahmad, there was no sign, despite extensive searches.

"If your son really loved you, he would not make you worry so," said one of his advisors, a horrible man who was hungry for power and wanted to break the sultan down so he could be in control of the kingdom.

The sultan tried not to take the advisor's words to heart, but it was difficult when he had no idea where Prince Ahmad was. And so, one day, he decided to call for a sorceress he had heard about, and tasked her with finding out all she could about Prince Ahmad's whereabouts.

The sorceress was a talented woman, and she tried everything she could to find Prince Ahmad. But despite using all her knowledge and tricks, she was unable to track his location.

"But," she said to the sultan on her return to him two days later, "while I can't find out where he is, I can sense that he is happy and content."

The sultan sighed; it would have to be enough for now.

What he wasn't to know was that Peribanou had seen her husband's sadness. When, after a few days, he still hadn't said anything to her, she gently asked him what was troubling him.

"I love our life," Prince Ahmad said slowly. "I

love you and being here with you, but my father is old, and I cannot help but want to see him and make sure he is OK."

Peribanou thought for a moment. She was reluctant to part from Prince Ahmad for any length of time, but she knew if her husband wasn't happy, she wouldn't be happy.

"Go and visit him," she said to Prince Ahmad, whose head shot up in surprise. "But you must promise me two things. Firstly, you must not tell him, or anyone else, that you are married to me. You must not mention me in any way, and you must not give even a hint of where it is you have been living. Humans can sometimes wish to take advantage of jinns and our powers, and I have no wish to put my people in danger. Secondly, you must promise to return to me."

Prince Ahmad immediately promised, and leaped up happily. Peribanou, delighted to see him so happy, laughed and called for preparations to be made for his journey.

The next day, Peribanou saw Prince Ahmad off. He was sat on a fine horse and was accompanied by a retinue of twenty horsemen.

As Prince Ahmad approached the city where he

had grown up, people began to recognize him, and soon a crowd had formed to line his way up to the palace. "Prince Ahmad, it's Prince Ahmad," called the crowd.

Their voices were heard by the sultan, who stood at the front door of the palace and watched as his youngest son approached. Prince Ahmad stopped his horse and leaped down, moving to kneel in front of his father. The sultan pulled him up to embrace him, and both men had tears of happiness spilling from their eyes.

After a long time, they separated and went inside, where Prince Ahmad told his father as much as he could about his journey to find the arrow, about finding it far away from the city. "I am married and happy," he concluded. "I cannot tell you anything else about my life, but know that I am happy."

It was all the sultan had wished for, and he asked no questions of his son, but simply requested that he visit again as soon as he possibly could. As he waved goodbye to Prince Ahmad, the sultan saw his advisor coming towards him.

"It is good that you have seen your son," the advisor said, "but don't you think it is quite strange that he won't tell you anything about where he's been?"

The sultan was too happy to let any negative words about Prince Ahmad affect him, and he went to sleep that night, secure in the knowledge that his youngest son was safe and well.

When Prince Ahmad returned to Peribanou, the fairy was ecstatic to see him. Although he had promised to return, there was still a part of her that worried. But life went back to the way it was before, and they were exceedingly happy.

Soon, though, Peribanou saw Prince Ahmad becoming sad at times. "What is the matter, my love?" she asked him one night over dinner.

Prince Ahmad sighed. "My father asked me to visit him again," he said. "I do want to go, but I don't want to leave you."

Peribanou laughed. "This is a problem that is easily solved," she said. "Every month, you will go and visit your father for three days, and on the fourth, you will return home to me. That's all there is to it."

And so that's what happened. The next day, Prince Ahmad went to the city, where his father greeted him with joy. After three days together,

Prince Ahmad returned to his home. And so it went, month after month. Each time he went, his retinue grew bigger and bigger and grander and grander.

This wouldn't have been a cause for concern, but the sultan's advisor was still trying to gain power, and after each visit by Prince Ahmad, the advisor would comment on how the prince had enough soldiers to overthrow his father. At first, the sultan didn't pay attention, but his son's secrecy about his home and his wife made him wary, and from there it was easy for the advisor to meddle and plant worries in the sultan's head.

Seeing as how she had been of great help before, the sultan called once more for the sorceress.

"When my son next visits, I want you to follow him and find out where he lives," he told her.

She agreed, and on Prince Ahmad's next visit, she followed his large retinue as it left the city. She skulked behind it for a number of parasangs, until she saw it make its way in between some large rocks.

She hurried forward, but when she got through the rocks, there was no one ahead of her. Somehow, all those men and all those horses had disappeared.

The sorceress looked around and found a path leading to an underground passage, but when she reached the end all she found was solid rock. Confused, she headed back to the city and to her home to come up with another plan.

A few weeks later found the sorceress back at the rocks where Prince Ahmad had disappeared, only this time she was lying on the floor. As she heard hooves approaching, she twisted her face into a look of agony.

Soon, Prince Ahmad caught sight of her and stopped, with his retinue behind him.

"Help," said the sorceress in a feeble voice. "I have fallen, and I can't get up."

Prince Ahmad swung down from his horse and knelt beside the woman. "If you put your arm around my neck, I will carry you on my horse to the city where we can get you medical attention," said the prince.

The sorceress let out a few (fake) sobs. "I am in so much pain," she wept. "I fear I cannot move any great distance."

There was only one thing to do; Prince Ahmad picked up the sorceress and walked with her to the passageway and through the iron door. He took her into the palace, and laid her on a bed in one of the many rooms, before hurrying away to find Peribanou.

After hearing what had happened, Peribanou followed Prince Ahmad back to the sorceress, who was still lying where she had been left. "I am told you are in great pain," said Peribanou. "Take this draught, it will help you sleep and while you sleep it will begin healing you."

Peribanou held out a small vial of liquid. Not wanting to look suspicious, the sorceress took it from her and did as instructed, and before long she fell into a deep sleep.

"Husband," said Peribanou, "you must continue on your journey and see your father as usual. I will look after this woman, and once she is better, will have her taken home to the city."

And so, Prince Ahmad left. Peribanou ordered two of her attendants to stay guard with the sorceress, and inform her when she woke up. The next morning, one of the attendants called for Peribanou, and she arrived to find the sorceress sitting up in bed and looking healthy.

"You must stay another day and make sure you are completely healed," said Peribanou.

But the sorceress was eager to get back to the city and tell the sultan what she had discovered. "No, no," she said. "I couldn't possibly trouble you any further. You've helped so much already."

Now, Peribanou's healing draught was good, but given how much agony the woman said she had been in yesterday, Peribanou was suspicious over how healthy she looked and how quickly she wanted to get away. Wanting to spend a little bit more time with her to work out what was going on, Peribanou offered to take her on a tour of the palace.

As they walked around, Peribanou caught sight of the greedy look in the sorceress's eyes, and knew that this woman was up to no good. Unable to delay the woman any longer, at the end of the tour she ordered a carriage to take the sorceress home. But Peribanou wasn't satisfied with leaving it there, and she asked two of her most faithful servants to trail the woman.

"Do not let her out of your sight," she told the women. "Record where she goes and who she speaks to, and if you can, listen in on her conversations, and then report back to me."

Upon her return to the city, unknowingly

followed by Peribanou's servants, the sorceress waited until she knew Prince Ahmad had left, and then hastened to see the sultan. There, in his study, she told him all she had seen.

"The palace is huge, ten times bigger than this one," the sorceress said. "And the fairy's guards are clearly well trained, and her power knows no bounds."

The sultan's advisor was also in the room, and he turned to the sultan. "It is only a matter of time before Prince Ahmad attacks us and tries to take over the throne," he said. "A man with that much wealth and power is always in need of more. You must protect yourself and the city from this fairy's powers."

The sorceress nodded in agreement. Faced with two of the people he trusted most warning him about his son, the sultan felt defeated. "What do you propose I do?" he asked them.

"Easy," said the advisor. "On his next visit, you must not allow Prince Ahmad to return home. He must be captured and thrown in the jail cells."

The sorceress scoffed. "That's a sure-fire way to bring an attack by the fairy down on us," she said. "And we won't win. What we need to do is make sure that Prince Ahmad goes away, and never comes back."

The advisor was unhappy, but saw the sorceress's point and was eager to hear her solution.

"Sultan," she said, "you must set the prince a challenge, and make him promise that if he cannot complete the challenge, he will leave the city and never, ever come back. Ask him to provide you with a tent large enough to house your whole hunting party, all the horses and dogs you take with you, and all the animals you capture. Surely, he will not be able to do this, and his failure will mean we never see him again."

So, the next month, when Prince Ahmad came to visit his father, the sultan took him aside. "I have asked you for little," he said, "but now I want something from you, and if you are unable to give it to me, you shall never return to this city, understand?"

When Prince Ahmad said he understood, the sultan explained what he wanted. Prince Ahmad was unsure he could fulfil the request, but when he told Peribanou, she was able to conjure what he wanted immediately.

"I am suspicious, though," she said, "of your

father's sudden request. There is something going on, and I have a feeling it is to do with the woman that you rescued and brought here. I had my people follow her after they returned her to the city, and as well as seeing her hurry to the palace, they also saw her meeting your father's advisor a number of times. I will keep an eye on her. Take the tent your father has requested, but be cautious."

The next month, Prince Ahmad presented his father with the tent. It was all folded up, and looked like a very small square of fabric, but when the sultan opened it, it covered the whole of the large gardens at the back of his palace. It would be more than big enough to hold his hunting party, even if they caught a forest's worth of animals.

Pleased, the sultan ordered the tent be folded up and carefully stored. He then turned to his son to explain the second challenge, which the sorceress and his advisor had explained to him the night before, just in case Prince Ahmad had succeeded in the first challenge. The pair had been plotting secretly together, outside of the palace, to come up with the challenges.

"Son," said the sultan. "I desire water be brought to me from the Lion's Spring. Can you do this for me? If you cannot, never come back to the city again."

Prince Ahmad promised his father he would try, but he despaired. The Lion's Spring was guarded by four lions, and at any one time two of them kept guard while two of them slept. All four were ferocious.

But Peribanou scoffed when she heard the challenge. From a box, she withdrew a ball of thread and gave it to her husband, along with an empty vial. "Take this thread," she said, "and make sure you follow all my instructions. First, you will need two horses. One is for you to ride, and on the other you will load a fresh mutton, split into four parts. Tomorrow, when you go through the gates of this castle, throw the ball of thread I have given you on to the ground. It will begin to unravel itself, and all you have to do is follow its path. When it stops, you will see four lions, and the two that are asleep will be woken by the other two on your arrival. Do not be afraid. Ride forward on your horse and, one at a time, toss the mutton quarters from the other horse on to the ground. The lions will be caught up in feasting on the mutton, and you will ride to the fountain, fill up the vial with water, and then turn around and ride back. No harm will come to you."

The next morning, Prince Ahmad woke up and set off, following Peribanou's instructions to the letter. While he was afraid at the sight of the lions, he knew Peribanou would never put him in danger, and he was able to get the vial of water without any trouble.

When he presented it to his father at his next visit, he could see the sorceress and his father's advisor looked displeased. The next morning, as he prepared to leave, his father came to him.

"Son, I have one final request of you," he said. "I want you to bring me a man who is seven feet tall. He must have a beard that is twenty arms long. On his shoulder, he must carry a quarter staff of steel that weighs five kilograms, but that he can move as easily as someone picks up and moves a fallen leaf. If you cannot find this man, never return to the city again."

The sorceress and the sultan's advisor were sure this would be an impossible challenge, and as Prince Ahmad made his way back him, he thought similar. But when he told Peribanou what had been asked of him, she simply smiled.

"You have never met him, but my brother, Shabbar, fits that description exactly," she said. "Many people are scared of him and turn away from him, but if you face him without flinching, you will have his loyalty for life."

Peribanou sent a messenger to her brother, and a couple of weeks later, he arrived at the palace. As he walked in to the throne room to greet his sister and her husband, Prince Ahmad made sure to look at him properly. He found nothing there to be afraid of and Shabbar, pleased the prince had looked at him openly, embraced his brother-in-law.

After spending a few days catching up, and hearing from Peribanou her suspicions about the sorceress and the sultan's advisor, Shabbar accompanied Prince Ahmad to the city.

As they rode through the city, many turned their faces away from Shabbar, afraid of his form. But when they saw the prince looking comfortable, they turned their heads back.

On arriving at the sultan's palace, Prince Ahmad led Shabbar into the throne room, where his father was waiting. Standing either side of his father were the advisor and the sorceress, and on seeing

Shabbar, they shied away from him, refusing to turn their faces back.

Offended, Shabbar brought the staff down from his shoulder and cut through the advisor and the sorceress. The sultan cried out in alarm.

"Father," said Prince Ahmad, moving forward to cup his father's shoulder with his hand. "Do not be afraid. This is my brother-in-law Shabbar, and all he has done is cut down those who were trying to manipulate you. The advisor and the sorceress were taking advantage of your old age and were trying to control you. But you have nothing to fear from them, or from me, now."

The sultan thought back over his interactions with the advisor and the sorceress, and saw them for what they were, telling lies about his son, who had done nothing but protect him and love him and fulfil his requests.

"My son," the sultan said. "Forgive me. As you have said, I am old and all this has done is show me that it is time for me to hand the reins over. I name you the next sultan, effective immediately."

Prince Ahmad was stunned, but accepted, on the condition that his father stay on and counsel him. He then sent messengers to Peribanou to tell her what had happened, and when his wife arrived at the palace, he introduced her to the sultan and the sultan decided to hand over the kingdom to them both.

From that day forth, Prince Ahmad and the fairy Peribanou ruled over the kingdom, peacefully.

# A Matter of Maths

## (INDIA)

This is a story about maths and, possibly, the invention of chess, or a game of strategy very like chess called chaturanga.

There are many versions of this story. In some, the man who brings the game to the king is a con man, while in others, the king is a cruel leader. In some, the king is already a fan of chess. In all of them, the key is not the game itself, although it may seem that way at first, but the board.

There is a legend associated with one version of the story, in which the king's opponent is the god Krishna who, when it becomes clear the prize is too big for the king to grant, tells the king that he must serve paal payasam, a type of sweet rice dish, to guests as payment of the prize. This is why paal payasam is still served by many people, including at the Ambalappuzha Sri Krishna Temple in Kerala.

Once upon a time, there was a king who ruled over a peaceful kingdom. There had been conflicts in the past, but the king was a clever leader and negotiator, able to work with the queens and kings of neighbouring kingdoms to avoid war. He was a fair and kind ruler, and his people were well fed. And so, with such a peaceful kingdom, the king, who was also a little bit competitive (OK, a lot competitive), had plenty of time to indulge in one of his greatest loves: games. He never wanted for games to play and, of course, being as skilled and clever as he was, he very rarely lost.

But the king was bored of playing the same games over and over again, and bored of winning, and bored of bad opponents, so he issued a challenge.

"Whoever brings me a new game to play, and whoever beats me at this game, shall be able to name his prize," the king's decree intoned.

The decree was spread far and wide across the land, into big towns and small villages. Farmers and merchants and students and cooks and tailors heard about the king's challenge, and all got to work on creating new games.

People came from far and wide to play against the king. They walked, and they came by horse.

They travelled in small groups, and they travelled alone. They were young and old, rich and poor. They brought board games, and games to play outside. They brought games that took over a whole room in the palace, and boards that took up a tiny space. They brought games played with cards, and games played with stones.

But each time, after they explained their game to the king, he would turn them away. "I have played a game like this," he would say. And so, disappointed, the people would leave.

One day, an unassuming looking man called Omar turned up at the palace gates. He had journeyed from a small town a long distance away, first walking, then catching a ride in a horse-drawn wagon, and then walking some more until he got to the palace. He was dressed simply, in a tunic and trousers. Under his arm, he carried a box decorated with black and white squares.

"I have come," said the man, "to play a game with the king."

The palace courtiers showed the man through to the throne room, where the king was sitting. The throne room was grand, with rich red carpet on the floor, and walls decorated in art, and, in one corner, a small table stacked with the king's favourite games.

The man bowed down before the king. "Your Royal Highness, my name is Omar and I have invented a new game which I wish to play with you," the man said.

The king was used to people saying this, and had little hope that the game was actually one he had never played before. But he believed in giving his subjects a hearing and waved for the man to come closer.

"This is a game of strategy, played using kings and queens and knights and pawns," said Omar.

The king was intrigued; he had not heard of a game like this before. But, not wanting to show his hand too early and then be disappointed, he waved the man on, urging him to continue his explanation.

"We play on this board," Omar said, holding out the box he had been carrying under his arm. "The figurines we use are black and white, and they can each only move in certain ways."

The king had never seen a board like it before, and he knew, at last, this was a new game.

"Very well," said the king. "Let us play this new game of yours."

The king got up from the throne and his servants and the man followed him to his game room. The room was spacious, and full of everything the king needed to comfortably play whatever game his heart desired. One wall was made completely of shelves, and on these were stacked dozens and dozens of board games. There was a chest of drawers, packed with dice of all different shapes, sizes and colours, as well as bags of marbles and counters. Around the edges of the room were tables, surrounded by cushions to sit on, while a big space in the middle was where the king played games that required a lot of movement. The walls were hung with tapestries depicting various games, as well as dartboards and even an archery board! It was an extraordinary space! Stepping into the room, the king sat down on a plush emerald-green cushion. When he was settled, a servant told the man to take his place opposite the king.

Omar sat down and opened the box, which contained a number of black and white pieces carved from wood. Setting the board between them, he lined up all the pieces and explained the rules to the king: which pieces could move in which direction, which pieces needed protecting, and what would mean a win.

The king nodded; he was a master strategist. After

all, he had protected his kingdom for years, working out the best strategies for when anyone tried to attack, ensuring his people had enough to eat, and that work and money were distributed fairly and equally.

The two men set about playing, with the king going first as he was playing with the white pieces. At first, it seemed like they were on an equal footing. "You're getting the hang of this well, Your Majesty," said Omar after the king had moved his pawn to a good position.

The king simply nodded, although inwardly he was not as calm. He was ecstatic to be playing something new, and he was even happier that the game was proving a challenge. He was having to carefully consider every move, and try and work out how it would affect moves he'd not yet even considered making. While his mind whirred, the king let the man take his turn. Soon, it became harder, with both men taking longer and longer to decide on their next move. Each slowly began to gather an equal number of the other's pieces.

Darkness came down, and the two men agreed to continue their game the next day. The king set a guard outside the room to ensure no one came in and moved the pieces in the night, although he'd already committed the entire layout to memory.

The next morning, the man joined the king in the game room again. They once more spent hours contemplating their moves, and for the first time ever while playing a game, the king felt nervous. Sweat began to gather at the back of his neck, and he started to question his every decision.

"I will move this one," said the king one moment, his hand hovering over a piece. But then he changed his mind. Humming, he let his hand drift over another piece. After holding it there for some time, he finally came to a decision, quickly moving the piece and then looking up at the man opposite him.

Omar smiled and reached his hand out for one of his pieces, swiftly moving it into a new position. The king knew immediately that Omar had won. He sat for a while, considering all his options, but whichever way he looked at it, he'd put himself in a corner and there was no way out.

Eventually, the monarch knocked over his king, and nodded at the man. "Congratulations," said the king. "As a reward for inventing a new game, and for besting me, you can name your prize."

The man thought for a moment. "I would like rice," he said. "I would like a grain of rice for the first square on my board, and then double for the second square, and then double again and so on."

The king was confused; the man's choice of prize seemed simple. "Are you sure you don't want jewels? Perhaps some emeralds and rubies for your loved ones?" the king asked. "Or maybe money? You could spend it on whatever you wished, or invest it. If you are a rider, I have some prime horses you could have? They are swifter than any other horses in the kingdom."

But the man insisted on his prize of rice. "Very well," said the king. "Servants, go and get me a bag of rice."

When the servants returned, they placed the bag of rice by the king and opened it. The king took out one grain and placed it on the first square. For the second square, he took out two grains. For the third, he took out four.

The king stopped. "Are you sure this is what you want?" he asked the man. "It seems like such a small prize, so I will give you one last chance to change your mind."

"I appreciate your thoughtfulness, Your Highness," said the man, "but I am content with my choice."

The king said nothing in return, but returned to

counting the rice, thinking that he wouldn't even get through a quarter of the bag.

But as he got further along the squares, the rice began to pile up. By the eighth square, he had put down one hundred and twenty-eight grains of rice, and they were spilling over the side. The king looked ahead, and, doing some quick maths in his head, realized that by square sixteen, he would have to put down more than thirty-two thousand grains of rice. And there were still six more rows of squares to go after that!

"It is too much rice for me to count," the king said to the man. "It is millions and millions of grains of rice."

The man nodded and smiled at the king.

"Ah," the king said, beginning to laugh. "You have brought me not one, but two new games, and beaten me at both!"

The king and the man laughed together, abandoning the counting of the rice. Instead, as reward for introducing the king to new games, the man was made a royal advisor. And he and the king played chess regularly.

# The Princess and the Salt

## (Afghanistan)

This story shares a beginning in common with another tale in this collection, "The Story of Prince Sobur", showing how variations of the same tale exist in various cultures across South Asia. There are even versions from England, Germany, Austria and more!

Some versions from Afghanistan include a little magic, but all, like this one, have love and loyalty at their core.

Once upon a time, there was a king who had three daughters whom he loved very much and who loved him in return. They lived happily in a small kingdom which the king ruled over firmly but fairly. He was not a cruel man, but he did not suffer fools, and was quick to anger sometimes.

One day, while they all sat together in the palace's dining room eating dinner, he asked them how they loved him.

"I love you like sugar," said the eldest daughter in a sweet voice, smiling widely, confident her father would love her answer.

The king was pleased, and turned to his middle daughter, who was always the peacemaker of the family. "I love you like honey," she said smoothly, smiling like her older sister.

The king smiled, and looked at his youngest daughter. She was secretly his favourite, as she reminded him of his late wife, who had always been keen on adventure and trying new things. "I love you like salt," she said, smiling like her sisters had.

The king was shocked. "Like salt?! You love me like salt?" he spluttered. He hoped that his daughter saw how ridiculous her answer was, so he gave her another chance to answer. "How do you love me?"

The youngest princess held her father's gaze. "I love you like salt, Father," she said clearly.

The king was not pleased. In fact, he was getting more and more angry. "How dare you say that?" he shouted, rattling the dishes and glasses on the table and causing his two older daughters to push themselves back from the table in fear.

"I dare to say it because it's true, Father," said the youngest princess, getting ready to explain her thinking.

But the king wouldn't let her speak any more. He gestured to his guards and said: "If my youngest daughter only loves me like salt, then she should not be in the palace. Escort her far away from here." And with that, he turned his back on his daughter and stalked out of the room.

The princess was upset, but knew there was no changing her father's mind. She bowed and then left the room, followed by two guards.

The princess changed into a simple, light blue gown, making sure to grab a cloak to keep her warm, and packed a bag, into which she put some of her plainest clothes. She stopped at the kitchens on the way out, where the kindly cook packed a bag of supplies, including sweet biscuits and breads and water.

And then, having said goodbye to her sisters, who were weeping, the guards escorted her to a forest close to the edge of the king's land, a day's walk away. There, they left her.

Although she was a princess and had lived in a gorgeous palace all her life, she was also brave and daring like her mother. She had persuaded the palace guards to teach her how to shoot a bow and arrow, and how to set traps for rabbits and small animals in the woods. She had camped outside in the woods many times before, and although she was nervous, she knew that the trees and animals would not hurt her.

Eventually, the princess began to get tired, so when she came across a big tree near a pond, she decided to settle there for the night. She built a fire to help her keep warm, and gathered water from the pond and figs from nearby bushes for her dinner to eat with the bread and butter the cook had packed. Then she wrapped her cloak around her and, using her bag as a pillow, fell asleep under the tree.

The next morning, the princess woke to see an old woman filling a large clay water pot at the pond. She leaped up and made her way over to the woman, who was stooped under the weight of the container. The old woman had silver hair, and was wearing a simple but well-made tunic and trousers, with a shawl draped over her head and shoulders. And although she was old, it was clear she was sprightly and quite strong, but the princess still knew she had to help an elder.

"Please, let me help you carry that," the princess said, taking the bottle from the old woman. "It's too heavy for you to take such a burden. I will carry it to wherever you would like."

"That is kind of you," said the woman. She noticed the bag under the tree and the princess's dishevelled hair. "Did you sleep here last night?"

The princess looked down nervously; she didn't want to tell the woman she was a princess. "Yes," she said, after a few moments of silence. "My name is Fatima. I have left home to make my way in the world, and I am still looking for somewhere to stay."

"Well," said the old woman, "you can carry that bottle of water back to my house and stay with me for a few days."

The princess grabbed her bag and the bottle,

and followed the old woman through the forest to a pretty cottage. There, the old woman made her a hearty stew of lentils, and the princess helped her clean up afterwards.

A few days passed, and the two got on so well that the old woman asked the princess to stay for a bit longer. Soon, the princess began to call the old woman grandmother, and the pair settled into a routine. Before they knew it, months had passed, with the princess helping the old woman with the tasks that were too hard for her to carry out, and the old woman teaching the princess how to cook, to sew, to grow things in the garden and more. As the seasons passed from summer into autumn into winter, the pair grew to love each other like they'd always been family.

One day, while the old woman was on her way back from her regular trip to the market to sell the vegetables that she and the princess had grown, and the crafted goods they had made, she came across a group of men. They were all dressed in the uniforms of soldiers from the palace, and when they parted, the old woman saw the king in their midst. She gasped and bowed low.

"Old woman," said the king, "my soldiers and I

have been out hunting, and we will soon require something to eat. Can you help?"

The old woman insisted the king and his soldiers come to her house, where she and her adopted granddaughter would cook for them. After giving directions, the old woman hurried back to the cottage.

"What has you so flustered?" said the princess when the old woman rushed through the door.

"I have just seen the king in the forest, and he and six of his soldiers will be here in an hour for dinner," said the old woman. "We must cook and clean. There is so much to do, Fatima."

The princess was surprised, but kept her face calm. This was an opportunity. "Do you trust me?" she asked the old woman.

"Of course," the old woman responded.

"Then I will take care of all the food," said the princess. "I will make a number of grand dishes for the king – a meat curry and samosas and a savoury chaat studded with pomegranate seeds – but I will also make our favourite simple and humble spinach dish."

The old woman hurried outside to set up a space for the king and his soldiers to eat, while the princess busily got chopping and stirring and sautéing and making the food.

When the king arrived, there were comfortable cushions set out on the floor outside the cottage, and a large space in the middle where a feast sat. Fragrant smells drifted up in the steam from the curries and rice and salads that were set on a low table the old woman had brought out from inside the cottage.

"This looks delicious," the king said, sitting down. His soldiers followed, and watched as the king reached for the grandest-looking dish. They were hungry too, and the chicken in a sauce with apricots looked good.

But when the king tasted it, he frowned. There was something not quite right. Shaking his head, he picked up the next dish, which looked scrumptious. But when he tasted that, he looked displeased. He tried all the dishes spread out in front of him, but none of them seemed to be to his taste. Perhaps the old woman and her granddaughter were bad cooks, and while that wasn't good, it also wasn't an offence. The king didn't want to shun the old woman's hospitality, so he continued on without saying anything.

The soldiers looked on, worried that the food was bad and they wouldn't get anything to eat after a long and tiring day in the forest. But their worry was nothing compared to the old woman's. *What has gone wrong?* she thought. *Usually anything Fatima cooks is excellent.* If the king hated everything he had been presented with, would he throw the old woman and Fatima into the dungeons?

The king came to the last dish: a simple spinach dish. As he tasted it, his soldiers and the old woman expected the same disappointed look as when he had tried the other foods. But instead, he let out a smile and began to dig in, and his soldiers followed suit.

When he had finished eating, the king turned to the old woman. "You provided a feast for me and my men," he said, "but all of the dishes tasted bland. The only one that was truly tasty was the spinach, and that was the simplest food you presented to me. I am puzzled as to why the other dishes did not taste as good."

Before the old woman could even think of anything to say, the princess stepped out from the cottage, where she had been watching and listening to the king as he ate his meal.

"Father," she said. The king turned to see his youngest daughter, and was so shocked he couldn't get any words out. "Remember that I told you I loved you like salt, and you threw me out, thinking it was an insult. But today, you have seen that salt is essential. All the dishes I presented to you were missing salt. And, despite the fact that they were grand dishes, you shunned them all for the simple spinach, the only dish that contained salt. And so, when I say I love you like salt, I mean that you are essential, and that without you, nothing feels quite right."

The king was humbled in the face of his daughter's explanation, and immediately regretted not giving her the chance to explain months before.

"Daughter, will you ever forgive me?" he asked. "I was too quick to assume, and too quick to look for flattery."

The princess, who had never stopped loving her father, stepped towards him and the two embraced for a long time.

"I forgive you, Father," said the princess. "And I would love to return home, but only if I can bring the old woman with me. She has taught me everything I know, including how to make all the food you saw before you today."

The king assented, and he, the princess and the old woman made their way back to the palace, accompanied by the soldiers. And every time the princess cooked after that, she always made sure to include salt.

# Manohara

## (SRI LANKA)

The Manohara is half woman, half bird, and is one of the heroes of the Jataka tales, a collection of stories and fables about the previous births of the Buddha in both human and animal form.

Versions of this story feature in the folklore of Sri Lanka, Myanmar, Laos, Cambodia and more, and a slightly different version can also be found in the folklore of China, Japan, Korea and Vietnam.

This story is documented in the stone reliefs at Borobodur, a ninth-century Mahayana Buddhist temple in Indonesia.

Once upon a time, in a kingdom very, very far from here called Kimnara, lived a princess. Her name was Manohara, and she was the youngest of the seven children of the Kimnara king. She and her six sisters lived on Mount Kailish, a land beyond the human realm.

It was a beautiful place to live, high up in the mountains where everything gleamed in slightly otherworldly colours: oranges and purples and blues that glistened and shimmered before the eye. The kingdom held music and song in high regard, and Manohara and her sisters were all talented at singing and playing multiple instruments.

But Manohara was a restless sort, and she wanted adventure in her life. So one day, she decided to travel to the human realm.

She made her way over mountains, across fields and lakes, past farmland and then into a dark, dense forest. The forest was full of animals, making it a perfect place for hunters who wanted to catch and sell things like deer.

On the day Manohara set foot in the forest, unbeknown to her, there was also a hunter there. He was there to capture animals, but when he saw Manohara he knew there was something special about her that could help him raise his station in life. He had worked as a hunter all his life, but he believed he deserved more, he deserved a life of luxury and pampering, and, being the selfish sort, he thought riches were due him at others' expense.

Realizing that Manohara was magic – he had an eye for that sort of thing and he could sense an aura about her – he got out his strongest tools and used all his cunning, following her carefully as she moved through the trees. When Manohara stopped at a stream for a drink, the hunter leaped out and threw his biggest net over her. She was so surprised that she couldn't move, giving the hunter the chance to quickly bind her wrists and feet with his strongest ropes.

When she was secured, the hunter journeyed with Manohara to the palace of King Adityavamsa and Queen Chandraderi, where he requested an audience with the royals.

In the throne room, the couple were joined by their son, Prince Sudhana. The hunter came before them, leading Manohara, whose wrists he had bound with special rope so she couldn't get away. Shocked by the attack, Manohara had decided she would wait and assess the situation before she rushed into action. *If I attack the hunter now,* she thought, *I could be attacked in turn by the soldiers in this palace. Better to try and escape later when there are fewer people around.*

The hunter bowed low, pulling Manohara down behind him. "Your Royal Majesties, Your Royal Highness," he said, bowing again to the king and queen and then to the prince. "I found this woman in the forest, and I would like to present her to you. I sense she is from another realm, and she could serve you well and help increase your dominion."

Now, in many other tales, the king, queen and prince might not hesitate to be so cruel as to accept the gift of a person. But King Adityavamsa and Queen Chandraderi had banned slavery as soon as they had ascended to the throne, and they had taught their son to have a similar respect for all life, no matter where someone came from, what they looked like, or how rich or poor they were.

"Free the woman," ordered the king. The hunter did so, thinking that he had pleased the royal family greatly. But before he had a chance to daydream about the titles and jewels he might be given, the king spoke again. "And take the hunter to the cells."

The hunter was stunned, as was Manohara, who looked on in confusion. "You," said the king, looking at the hunter, "know that slavery is outlawed in this realm, and that people are not belongings to be exchanged or given as presents. I find you guilty of going against the laws of the realm, and sentence you to six years in prison."

The guards led the hunter, who was speechless, out of the room, and the royal family turned their attention to Manohara, who was still standing before them.

"What is your name?" asked Queen Chandraderi gently. "And where have you come from? We will make sure you return safely to your family."

"I am Manohara," came the reply. "My family live far away, and I am on an adventure, seeking to learn more about the world. I don't want to go back home yet."

"In that case," said the queen, "I insist you stay with us in the palace. Son, show Manohara to the north wing – she can take those as her quarters. If you need anything, Manohara, you only need to say."

Prince Sudhana led Manohara to her rooms, which were big but comfortable and cosy. Over the coming days, she settled in, getting to know the rhythms and routines of the palace.

Soon, Manohara began venturing further out, and

seeing her interest, Prince Sudhana offered to show her more of the realm. They spent long days riding to nearby towns and villages, where Manohara interacted with the people. From one, she learned to intricately embroider clothing, spending days working on a dress she eventually presented to the queen to thank her for her kindness and hospitality. In a larger town, Manohara asked the blacksmith to teach her how to forge a sword. After hours over hot flames, she and the blacksmith produced a sword with a beautifully carved handle.

"This," said Manohara, handing the sword to Prince Sudhana at the end of the day, "is for you."

The prince was a little stunned, and tried to push the sword back to Manohara. "You've spent so long working on it, you should keep it for yourself," he said.

But Manohara insisted, and in the end, Prince Sudhana took the sword and hung it in pride of place on the wall of his chamber. Every time he looked at it, he was reminded of the time he spent with Manohara and it put a smile on his face.

After so many weeks and months touring, Manohara settled on her favourite thing to do: painting, with Prince Sudhana by her side. The pair would often ride out and find a pretty view – a lake, a forest, a meadow – and spend time sketching and exchanging stories about their lives. It took Manohara a while to find her rhythm, but soon she moved from sketches and finished her first painting of her and Prince Sudhana's favourite spot: a field filled with flowers and butterflies and birds, dappled in sunshine.

Before long, it was clear the pair were in love. And so they decided they would marry. Their wedding was a happy occasion for the realm, but their ceremony was intimate and small, with just their closest friends in attendance, as well as the king and queen.

But while Prince Sudhana and Manohara had been falling in love, there were forces in the kingdom that weren't happy. One of the royal counsellors was annoyed at the pair's love and their popularity, and he knew that it put his own role in the kingdom at risk. And so he had been conspiring with a nearby kingdom, passing on unfounded rumours that King Adityavamsa wanted to overthrow his neighbours and take over their throne. It had taken a long time, but the neighbouring kingdom had decided to try and infiltrate the edges of the land.

A battle was brewing and Prince Sudhana knew he had to lead his army to try and stop harm from coming to his people.

"I will be back very soon," he told Manohara as he removed the sword she had made him from the wall.

Manohara sighed. "Do you have to go at all?" she asked. She knew the answer, and she would never stop him from going, but she was worried nonetheless.

"I doubt we'll even fight, it will probably just be a lot of posturing," the prince said, to try and comfort her. "I owe it to my people to defend our land. But I also owe it to you to return unharmed, and I promise to do that, my love."

Prince Sudhana took Manohara's face gently in his hands and turned it up so that their eyes met. "I promise," he said again.

Manohara nodded. "I'll hold you to that promise," she said. "I love you."

And so Prince Sudhana left for the border, accompanied by a regiment of soldiers.

While he was gone, the royal counsellor turned his attention to Manohara. He began by implying that the neighbouring kingdom was unhappy at Manohara and Sudhana's marriage, because the prince had been promised to the next kingdom's princess (this was, of course, completely untrue).

"Ah, Princess Manohara," he would always begin. "You know that I like you, but a great insult has been done to the neighbouring realm, and I worry that soon our people will also begin to see the danger your marriage to Prince Sudhana puts us all in."

At first, Manohara was able to ignore the counsellor's stirring, but soon he was telling her that she brought bad luck to the kingdom and, missing the prince and thinking he should have been back by now, her defences were down and his words – filled with their subtle digs – got to her.

"Do you really think Prince Sudhana could be hurt because of me?" she asked the counsellor one day.

"Ah, Princess Manohara," he said in his silky voice. "It's not really your fault because you didn't mean to bring bad luck to the kingdom, but it's strange that, after so many years of peace, it's just after your arrival that things start to go badly. I'm sure Prince Sudhana will be fine, but if he's not, then I expect you'll feel terrible."

And so, after agonizing alone for days, Manohara decided to secretly leave the kingdom and return home to her own realm. Before going, she left behind a ring only Prince Sudhana would recognize, in a place only he would think to look. Alongside this, she left directions to the Kimnara kingdom. And then, in the dead of night, she left.

Calling on her magic, she transformed herself into a bird of the sort humans had never seen, with a speed unmatched by anything from the human realm. She flew over valleys and mountains and through the skies to return to her home, where she was greeted by her father and sisters.

"And that's what happened," she said a couple of hours later, ending the story of her trip to the human realm, her love for the prince and her decision to leave. Her father saw the devastated look on her face and knew his daughter was mourning the man she'd left behind.

"If he loves you," he told Manohara, "then he will work out your signals and come to find you. You must have hope, daughter."

If Manohara had stayed in the human realm for just two more days, she would have seen Prince Sudhana return home, completely safe. He had managed to negotiate with the neighbouring kingdom and, in talking to the ambassadors sent to meet him in the hope of finding a peaceful solution, discovered his counsellor's machinations.

Once he'd arrested the counsellor, Prince Sudhana hurried to his quarters to greet Manohara, but she was nowhere to be found. The palace servants hadn't seen her in a couple of days, and nor had his parents. All of them assumed others had spoken to her.

As everyone searched the palace, the prince returned to his and Manohara's rooms. He looked around and his eyes caught on a painting Manohara had created and given him of their favourite spot. Taking it off the wall, he turned it around and saw the ring and note secured to it. Reading it, he knew he had to make his way to the Kimnara kingdom immediately.

Remembering from his talks with Manohara while they painted that only animals knew the way to the Kimnara kingdom, Prince Sudhana sought out a hermit he knew could speak to animals. For months, the hermit patiently taught the royal how to speak to creatures of all kinds. During this time, the prince also learned a series of prayers he would need to perform to win back the princess.

And then, the prince set off properly on his journey, regularly speaking to various animals for directions. One day, a pair of birds told him that an ogre was up ahead, blocking the path. The prince cautiously approached, peeking out from some trees and seeing the ogre, who was twice his height and width, up ahead. The path was bordered on either side by tall rocks, so the only way ahead was straight past where the ogre stood.

Prince Sudhana retreated to think about what he should do, and take stock of his weapons and belongings in case anything could help. In his bag, he found a pair of cowbells. Knowing that ogres loved eating cows, more than they even loved eating humans, he came up with a simple plan.

The prince hid his belongings close to the path, just out of sight of the ogre, and then went into the woods to find a good tree, from which he hung the cowbells, sure they would catch the breeze.

Then he returned to the path and stepped fully on to it, making sure the ogre could see him. Prince Sudhana began breathing heavily, as though he had been working very hard. Not giving the ogre a chance to make a move, the prince spoke: "That blasted cow!"

At his shout, the ogre perked up – there was a cow nearby? He loved cows; they were so delicious.

"I am sick and tired of dragging that cow behind me," Prince Sudhana continued, seeing he'd caught the ogre's attention. "I would give it to someone for free if they would just take it off my hands."

"I'll take it," shouted the ogre. The prince started,

as if he hadn't realized anyone else was there. "I'll take it," the ogre said again. "How do I find it?"

The prince smiled; the ogre had fallen perfectly into his trap. "All you need to do is follow the sound of the cowbells, and you'll find the cow tied to a tree," the prince said.

The ogre hurried off, following the tinkling of the cowbells. They grew louder and louder until the ogre stepped into a clearing, which was completely empty. Puzzled, for he was sure this was where the sound was coming from, he looked around and saw the cowbells hanging from a tree, swaying in the breeze and tinkling lightly.

Realizing he'd been tricked, the ogre growled and hurried back to the path, but it was too late. Prince Sudhana had grabbed his hidden belongings and run down the path, getting too far away for the ogre to chase him.

The prince continued on for many, many, many months, getting directions from the animals, and facing more challenges, including crossing a river of flames. He'd had to fashion himself a pair of leather shoes from a deer he hunted down, and then he hopped his way across the flames, looking rather silly and glad that no one was around to see him! In total, the journey took him seven years, seven months and seven days.

Finally, weary but excited at the thought of seeing the love of his life again, he arrived in the Kimnara kingdom, where he was greeted by the king. The prince performed the prayers he had learned to win back the princess.

"I have heard a lot about you from my daughter," said the king. "She has been waiting a long time for you to come to see her, and although you have done well to get here and you have performed the correct prayers, I will need you to take some tests to ensure you are worthy of her."

The prince immediately agreed and underwent three tests, which the king and Manohara had decided on together. He lifted a stone bench in the garden, which demonstrated his strength. As she watched him, Manohara knew this would be the easiest of the three tasks.

Then he had to show his skill with a bow and arrow, perfectly hitting three targets, showing his patience and precision. *This will test him*, thought Manohara. *He can sometimes be impatient, and he will need to wait for exactly the right moment to let those arrows go.*

She needn't have worried. During his long travels,

Prince Sudhana had learned to be patient, and he took his time with the arrows, lining up his view perfectly and only letting go when the wind had settled. Each of the three times he fired, his arrow landed perfectly in the centre of the target.

The final task saw Prince Sudhana blindfolded; he had to identify Manohara from among her sisters, just by touching her hand, in a demonstration of his faithfulness and knowledge. *I know he loves me,* thought Manohara, as she and her siblings lined up together. *He could pick my voice out of a crowd, and he could spot my hair from a mile off. But will he know me from a brief touch of our hands while he can't see?*

But when he gripped Manohara's hand, the prince immediately knew he was holding his beloved's hand. He raised it in the air.

Manohara took off his blindfold and the pair embraced, both breathing a sigh of relief at being together again at the end of such a long and testing period apart. The king blessed their marriage, and the Kimnara kingdom celebrated.

And the pair lived happily ever after.

# The Jogi's Punishment

## (INDIA)

*This story originally appeared in* The Lilac Fairy Book
*by Andrew Lang.*

Once upon a time, a young jogi – a religious man – arrived in the city of Rahmatabad. There, he took up residence under a tree, where he sat doing his devotions and reading prayers.

At first, people only visited him because they were curious – the city didn't have many jogis – but soon word began to spread about how people had had good luck after receiving a blessing from him. A few people turned into dozens, and dozens turned into a flood. He enjoyed having people visit him, because in return for blessings they gave him food and money.

Given his growing popularity, it wasn't long before the rajah of Rahmatabad heard about the religious man and began visiting him too. After a few trips, the king decided that he wanted the jogi to only serve him.

He set about building a shrine for the man, with a couple of rooms attached for living quarters.

"This place is all yours," the rajah said to the jogi, "but you are only to see me and the queen, and a few students you have handpicked to teach."

The jogi, who was happy at the prospect of a comfortable life paid for by someone else, agreed and moved in, spending his days teaching his pupils and talking to the king whenever he visited.

Now, the king had a daughter and it wasn't long before she heard about the jogi. A naturally curious sort, she kept her ear to the ground and fostered a good relationship with all the workers in the palace, who she heard talking about the man.

Of course, she was desperate to visit him and get a blessing, but there was just one problem: the princess wasn't allowed out of the palace on her own, and she certainly wouldn't be allowed to visit the jogi. The king had long ago betrothed her to the prince of the neighbouring kingdom of Dilaram, and he expected his daughter to stay in the palace until her wedding.

The princess, as we have heard, was curious and also a little rebellious. She wasn't going to marry some man she didn't know, but she'd solve that problem when it came time for her to meet the prince and marry. First, there was another problem to solve: how was she going to get out of the palace to visit the jogi?

After a few days of keeping watch, the princess figured out the perfect time and route to leave the palace unseen. Taking a cloak to help her disguise herself, she snuck out into the darkness and made her way to the jogi's house.

When she arrived, the jogi took one look at her

and fell suddenly in love. "Have a seat," he said to the princess, holding out his hand to her.

But the princess, who was very clever and intelligent, noticed the greedy look in the jogi's eyes and turned and ran away as fast as she could. She was a very, very fast runner and although he tried, the jogi couldn't catch up with her. Stopping in the town square, he spotted a lance leaning against a wall and, taking it up, threw it in the direction of the princess.

"Ow!" the princess exclaimed. It had caught her in the leg, but there was no time to waste. She pulled it out quickly and continued on the journey home.

When she arrived back at the palace, the princess snuck in and ran herself a bath. Carefully cleaning her wound, she bandaged it well, hoping it would heal before anyone – especially her father – noticed.

The next day, the king went to visit the jogi, but instead of finding him in his usual chatty mood, the jogi was sullen and quiet.

"What is the matter?" asked the rajah. The jogi said nothing, so the king tried again: "If you talk to me, I can help. I am the king after all."

"There is nothing you can do to help with this problem," said the jogi, who had been up all night thinking about how the princess had got away. His pride was hurt, and he was angry about it. He wanted revenge. "You will not like what I have to say."

The king protested: "Whatever you have to say, I will listen to it."

And so the jogi, who had come up with a plan overnight, began to speak: "There is a creature in this city that has the ability to destroy everyone in the palace." He paused and watched with delight as horror dawned over the king's face. "This creature is an evil spirit and it has taken over the body of a young woman," the jogi continued. "It came to visit me last night, and transformed into a hideous beast with sharp claws and teeth and rough skin as it attacked me. Luckily, I was able to wound it in the leg. Whichever woman you find with a lance wound on her leg, she is the evil spirit in disguise."

The king immediately ordered his soldiers to go house to house and examine the leg of every woman for a wound. His own household was not exempt, and so it was not long before the princess was discovered with her bandaged leg. The king didn't want to believe his daughter was an evil spirit, but when none of the other women of the kingdom were found to have a wounded leg, he had to resign himself.

The king went to speak to the jogi about the

discovery. "But surely there is some mistake," he said, after telling the jogi his daughter was the only one with a wound. "Are you sure it was the leg where she was hurt?"

The jogi was prepared for the king's reluctance, and said: "I have always spoken the truth to you, and if you choose not to follow my advice in this matter, there is nothing I can do to save you."

Afraid, the king agreed to follow the jogi's instructions, and so sent for two carpenters. They constructed, on the jogi's instructions, a wooden box big enough to hold a human. Once shut, clever mechanisms on the box meant it couldn't be opened from the inside.

When the box was ready, the jogi and the rajah took it to the palace in the middle of the night. Then, the king called for his daughter. When she arrived, having hurried because she was surprised to get a summons so late, the jogi and the king grabbed her to try and put her in the box. It wasn't easy. She struggled hard, kicking out to try and escape. But eventually the pair overpowered her and got her in the box, quickly securing the lid. And then they dragged the box – with some difficulty because the princess was still trying to get free from inside – down to the river, and threw it in.

Returning to his home, the jogi called for his two most loyal students. "The two of you should go down to the river where it comes out the other side of the forest," he said to them. "Wait there, and in a day or two a large wooden box should come floating by. Grab the box from the river, and bring it back to me."

The students, who were so loyal they would never question anything the jogi said, headed down to the river.

As the next day dawned, a little further upriver there was a huge crowd of people: it was the prince of Dilaram and his retinue. They were out hunting when the prince spotted the box floating on the water.

"Quick," he said to a few of his soldiers, "wade into the water and get that box."

The soldiers did as he said, and soon stood dripping water on the shore, having placed the box in front of the prince. Looking carefully all around, he spotted a mechanism and twisted it, getting the box open. Peering down into it, he jumped back in shock when he spotted a woman lying there, asleep.

Gasps rose up from the prince and his retinue, waking the princess up. A little disoriented by the light, she blinked a few times and then slowly unfolded herself from the box, standing up and taking in the sight of all the people around her.

She climbed out of the box and looked at the prince. "Who are you?" she asked.

"I am the prince of Dilaram," he replied, bowing to her.

The princess gasped. "I am the princess of Rahmatabad," she said.

The prince's eyes widened, realizing what was happening: that they were betrothed to each other and were finally meeting. But there would be time to deal with that later, and deal with it they would, because the prince didn't want to marry someone he didn't know. First, the prince knew the princess needed food and water, and a doctor to look over her to check she was OK.

"Something terrible has clearly happened to you," he said. "Will you come back to the palace with me to recover and tell us your story?"

The princess agreed, and when they arrived at the prince's home, she had a bath and got changed, and a maid helped her change the bandage on her wounded leg. Then she made her way to the banqueting hall, where the prince waited with his parents, and a feast.

"Sit," said the queen. "Have some food, and when you have satisfied your appetite, tell us your story."

The princess tucked into some freshly baked bread, homemade cheese and a dish of aubergines and tomatoes. Once she had eaten a few bites, she began to speak, telling the trio how she had snuck out of the palace to see the jogi, the chase and her injury, and how her father and the jogi had trapped her in the box.

The king, queen and prince reacted with horror and indignation at what had happened. "I know the rajah well," the king said, "and I am shocked he has treated you this way. You are welcome to stay here for as long as you like. You will be safe and free to do whatever you please."

Meanwhile, the prince had been thinking and had come up with a plan. "We still have the wooden box," he said. "I will trap a large, fierce monkey in it and put it back on the river in the hope that the jogi will want the box returned to him."

So that's exactly what he did, and the next morning the jogi's students, who had been getting bored watching the river, spotted the box their master had told them about.

248

Dragging it out of the river and back to the jogi's house, they deposited it at his feet in his room. Turning to his students, he addressed them in a firm voice: "You are to stand here, outside my door, and you are not to disturb me at all." And then he turned, walked into the room and shut the door behind him.

The pupils heard the jogi open the box, and then there was a huge shriek. The students looked at each other in alarm, but their instructions had been to stand by the doors, and that's what they were going to do.

From the room came the sounds of furniture crashing and more shrieking, and then the door was thrown open and the jogi ran past them, followed by a clearly very angry monkey. The jogi had discovered a reason to run fast, and he sprinted all the way out of the kingdom to avoid the monkey, and was never seen again.

When news reached Dilarum, the king called his old friend the rajah to him. When the rajah arrived, he was shocked to see his daughter, and fell at her feet asking for forgiveness, for the jogi's abandonment of the kingdom – plus the story of the students – had enlightened him to the jogi's true nature.

The daughter shared her story with the rajah, and the rajah shared his in return, and his daughter forgave him.

"But," the princess said to her father, "you must allow me to pursue my own life and my own adventures. I am strong and able to survive on my own, and there is much of the world I want to see. And I want to be released from my betrothal to the prince."

For the first time, the king truly looked at his daughter and saw a courageous and independent woman, The princess no longer had to marry the prince of Dilarum, and she set off on a trip around the world. And during that trip, she and the prince exchanged long letters, getting to know one another. When she returned, maybe they got married, and maybe they didn't. Either way, it was their decision.